Devil's Breath

J. Karon Roberts

ISBN: 9798587121645

Dedication

I dedicate this book to my dear friend and mentor, Pastor Steve Diamanti. We have known each other for eleven years and I had the privilege of attending his wedding.

His ability in many areas made him the perfect choice to edit this book. Steve is a strong Godly man with great integrity.

He lovingly poured through my manuscript to make the necessary corrections.

The book you hold in your hands is the result of Steve's unwavering dedication to helping others. I am honored to be called his friend and sister in Christ.

Acknowledgements

First and foremost, I give God all the glory for the honor of writing this book series. At an early age, he placed in me a love for words.

After graduating from the ***School of Hard Knocks***-I think I have a ***Ph.D.***- I fell in love with Jesus and He placed my feet on His road to glory in heaven.

I thank my family for putting up with the years of inferior writing but still sat and listened to me.

I thank my readers, who bless me and deem my work valuable. Your unwavering support has kept me on the path I am now on.

Finally, I would be remiss if I did not acknowledge Deer Lodge Assembly in Deer Lodge, Montana where I am a member.

My church family gives me the unconditional love and support needed to stay in and follow God's will. I love you all.

Forward

I have known Karon for a few years now, and I have seen her go through quite a few trials and tribulations. But, through them all she has never wavered in her faith in God. This is reflected in her writings and the storyline of this book.

She has an uncanny ability to take facts (medical, military, and scientific, etc.) and meld them with current issues we are all facing today. Karon takes all this information and weaves them into an exciting story.

This writing takes us on a fictional adventure and journey that could very well come to pass in real life today. This is a harbinger of things to come.

Throughout the whole story, Karon shows how God is ever-present in our lives. We just need to trust in Him and not try to lean on our own understanding, but allow Him to guide our path (Proverbs 3:5,6) and He will get us through every trial we find ourselves in.

As you read this story you will move back and forth from one scenario to another, each with its own highs and lows. You will find yourself anxiously waiting to turn the page or go to the next chapter to find out what is happening to the characters in the story.

Once you start on this path of reading this book, you will find yourself not wanting to put it down until you finish the story. It captivates your curiosity and imagination.

Karon completes this story leaving me anxiously waiting for the sequel. Enjoy this book and do not forget the message it portrays. Happy reading!

Pastor Steve S. Diamanti

Contents

Chapter 1: *Encounter*

David Garner had no idea he was about to take a journey, one that would change his perspective on everything. God's messenger is about to change David's life forever.

The Seattle skyline was dim and grey as the April morning ushered in new rainfall. Streetlights were still burning because of the dark clouds hanging over the city. The rolling hills had given birth to crocus flowers. Their bright purple colors dotted the landscape everywhere. Growing wild, they appear wherever the soil allows. This flower is the first sign in the Northwest that spring is eminent.

Rainwater trickled down the hills, gaining speed to the drains below, before dumping back into the Puget Sound. Ferries were pulling in and out, moving cars and passengers to and from the port.

Vashon Island had its route to deliver the residents to Seattle. Most left their vehicles on the island and chose to be foot traffic aboard the ferry and catch a bus to their respective jobs. It was much cheaper than paying the more significant fee for the car every day.

The city wakes up to the sounds of garbage trucks, buses, and locals. Streets were crowded with pedestrians racing to catch their bus to work. Some headed for the subways where electric buses were converted to gas, to travel to Bellevue, Ballard, and Mercer Island, and other outlining areas.

The streets soon filled with cars, with drivers ebbing their way to work. The Interstate 5 freeway was the main artery in and out of town and regularly became clogged by many vehicles. Even the express lanes made little difference.

Commuter trains from Tacoma to Seattle eased the I-5 congestion but only a little. The Super Rail from Rainier Valley traveled to Seattle International Airport-SeaTac- helped relieve the already congested city.

Some commuters traveled to the airport from the Park and Ride parking lots above the Kent valley and hopped a bus the rest of the way to downtown. It was cheaper than paying for parking, where charges could be as high as twenty dollars a day. That was the human side of life.

Nature was far more tranquil in their daily pursuits. Robins were busy harvesting the worms which had surfaced from the rain. Birds sang as they communicated with their mates. Robins, Sparrows, Mallards, and wild geese all warbled in the noisy din. A tiny bird was tugging on a worm, trying to escape becoming the morning meal.

The nightlife in Seattle was never quiet. Sirens blared from police cars, fire trucks, or ambulances all night long. It was more reassuring to the residents that they were protected. Few lost any sleep over it.

The rain tapped against David's bedroom window, waking him to its morning melody. He turned and looked at his clock and it was 6 a.m. Monday morning advanced too soon, but David welcomed it. He listened to the rain and the birds singing.

It was a sweet welcome, which morning brings.

David looked around his bedroom, admiring the architecture of his new home which was built in the 1950's. He took his time finding the right one. As an architect, David knew every facet of the building trade, and loved the wrap around porch and the curved arches inside the house.

He found this perfect place on Queen Anne Hill, which bordered the Fremont District, close to his business.

He knelt by his bed and thanked God for his countless blessings. The melody of his feathered companions was a sweet background to his prayer. David's heart flooded with joy, peace, and thankfulness as he thought of all the ways God had blessed him.

After his morning shower, he dressed, fixed his coffee, breakfast, ate, and went into his study, and took his bible and read for an hour. It was his God time.

His father was a pastor and taught David that the only way to have a good day, no matter what, was to begin each day with his heavenly Father. That way, he could handle anything unexpected which might arise. David took him seriously.

He owned Skyline Architectural Firm and was excited to begin a new day. His dream was to be an architect and work at what he loved.

David remembered back in March, receiving a call from General William Casey, "Billy," who lived in Albuquerque, New Mexico. The two met in his office a week later to discuss General Casey's plans. It was a multi-million-dollar project which would raise David's firm to world-class status. David was excited.

Casey and David enjoyed talking about God and their mutual faith in Jesus, but Billy did not tell David that he knew of him through others, but he hired his firm after meeting him.

In the last week in March, General Casey sent photos to David of the hunting lodge so David could work on the remodel. He was pleased to see that the building already had solar panels, which meant they were self-sufficient in case of power outages.

For the next three weeks, David worked diligently preparing the lodge's plans. He sent a copy via a secure email to the General, who was happy with the results. David would do final preparations on site.

He knew that he would be living there temporarily to augment the plans, so he went to the Christian agency, which specialized in finding professional house sitters. He interviewed several couples and chose the pair closest to his beliefs.

General Casey found a condo fully furnished just a few miles away from the lodge. He also leased a 2019 Subaru Outback for David to use while he was there.

April 17th was the day both agreed for David to arrive. He had seven days to orchestrate his move and leave his house in capable hands.

David instructed his manager regarding the projects that were still in the hopper. He had complete confidence in Shawn that he would run the firm with the same integrity he demonstrated. He left work early, since the weather was warmer in Albuquerque, so he could buy new clothes for the trip.

He called his brother John, to reassure him that his move was temporary. The call went to voicemail. So he left a message. John called David back and invited him to dinner. It would be the last time they would get together before leaving.

David chose to go after April 15th so he could make sure his accountant would have everything needed to submit the firm's tax statements, as well as his own.

The day came and went with no problems, and he handed off the firm to Shawn on the 16th of April so David would have time to pack and brief the house sitters.

He retired early, hoping to get some much-needed sleep. David had to be out of his house by 4:30 a.m. to make it to Sea-Tac Airport for his 6:10 flight. But like most travelers, David was no exception. He tossed in fitful sleep, waking up hourly to look at his clock.

At 3:00 a.m., he gave up and headed to the shower. God's time was his only priority, and he decided to feed on God's word instead of filling his stomach. The first-class flight offered breakfast, so he just had coffee with God and enjoyed their communion together.

The airport shuttle arrived at 4:10 to pick him up. Since David was traveling first-class, he could have two bags to check for free and his carry-on.

He arrived at Sea-Tac Airport at 4:50 am., which gave him plenty of time to check-in. Another perk for first-class travelers was the express lane through security; however, the first-class lounge was not yet open.

David took the subway to an Alaskan airline gate on the other end of the terminal. It was 5:20 a.m., and the ticket agent was already at the check-in counter, helping a few early passengers with seat assignments. The line was short, and David moved quickly to the counter.

The agent took David's ticket and boarding pass, validating his arrival. She showed him where he could sit in the first-class area.

It was 5:40 a.m. Ticket holders with first-class tickets boarded the plane first. David's seat was A-1, which placed him in a window seat. The world always seemed much smaller from the air. He loved looking out the window at the landscape below and experiencing God's majesty. His creation of the plains, the mountains, and the oceans was all breathtaking.

###

The plane landed in Albuquerque, New Mexico, at 2:41 p.m., right on schedule. A limo driver held a sign with David's name on it, and the two walked to the baggage claims.

The driver placed the bags in the back of the vehicle and drove the 10 miles to David's leased condo. He carried David's bags inside the apartment, handed him the keys to his temporary domicile and car, thanked him, and left.

The modern industrial furniture made David feel at home. He went into the kitchen and opened the refrigerator.

It was full of steaks, pork chops, and chicken. There were also plenty of frozen vegetables he liked. There was even ice cream.

David took his suitcases into the master bedroom, hung up clothes, put the folded ones in the dresser, and took the toiletries into the bathroom.

He took his carry-on and computer bag and placed his computer in the office. He purposely kept his Bible in his pouch in case there were any travel delays so he could read it. It rested to the right of the computer. He stowed the suitcases in the office closet.

Everything was unpacked and put where he wanted it.

David could feel his fatigue taking control. His sleepless night was reminding him to rest. His phone rang, and General Casey was on the other end.

"Did you have a good flight, David?"

"I did, but the night before was restless."

"I know what you mean. It's called travel anxiety, or that's what I call it anyway. I know you are tired, but I wanted to make sure your place was stocked with plenty of food and furnished exactly right."

"Thanks, General, everything is great."

"Around here, the locals know me as Old Billy, so call me Billy. I'll let you unwind and will see you tomorrow at 3:00 p.m., okay?'

"Thank you, Billy; I'll see you tomorrow." David hung up.

It was going on four o'clock, and David was getting hungry. He went to the kitchen found a New York steak in the fridge, pulled it out with a premade salad. He opens the cupboard above the stove and finds all kinds of spices.

'This man does not forget anything.' He thought.

After dinner, he settled into his office chair and examined the lodge's final drawings. It was a significant undertaking and could take months to complete. He was pleased with his designs and hoped Billy would also approve. Hours passed.

He remembered the ice cream in the freezer and grabbed a bowl, a spoon, and a scooper and dished himself up a healthy serving of Moose Tracks with salted caramel.

Relishing every bite, David finished it, went back to the kitchen, rinsed the dishes, and place them in the dishwasher. Again, fatigue was knocking at his door.

It was eight-thirty, so he changed into his pajamas. It had been a long day, and the setting sun was waning descending behind the mountains.

David would spend his first night in his condo. He brought his Bible into the bedroom and read it before bed. He was unaware of what morning would bring.

'Thank you, grandpa, for this beautiful Bible.' He thought.

As he thumbed through the pages, he would stop where he found writing in the margins. He was always amazed at how wise grandpa was in discovering the truths of God. He cherished his gift.

It was dog-eared and had notes in the margins, and certain places were underlined or highlighted. New book tabs replaced the old, at least twice.

In the book of Acts, he read about the apostle Phillip, who brought the Ethiopian eunuch to Jesus, which read:

"When they came up out of the water, the Spirit of the Lord suddenly took Phillip away, and the Ethiopian did not see him again but went on his way rejoicing." (Acts 8:39).

David took the attached ribbon and placed it between the pages he had just read. God had taken Phillip physically and spiritually away.

He contemplated if it could happen today and was comforted knowing that God had it all worked out and would reveal it in due time.

Putting his Bible on the nightstand, David slid between the cool cotton sheets. A peaceful rest coaxed him to sleep. He began to dream that God was showing him present and future events.

The dream began as if he had just gone to bed; a typical night like so many nights passed. This night was anything but ordinary. As he lay on his back in rem sleep, images began to emerge.

The stench of sweat, smoke, and gunpowder hung in the air. David slowly opened his eyes. He lay face down in the dirt and debris.

Did David jerk awake, or did he dream it, or was he somehow moved by the Holy Spirit and shown the future? It made him feel like he is living it and it was real.

Is it possible to be taken and brought back to the body through the Holy Spirit?

Pain brought him to consciousness. The smoke cleared, and David could see the ruins around him. Warm blood drooled down the right side of his face.

'Where am I?' he thought.

David saw his furnished condo in the rubble of bricks and broken mortar. He sat up to assess the situation. His car had taken a direct hit from a falling chimney, flattening it.

Not seeing his bicycle, he assumed it had been stolen by looters, although it too could have been destroyed.

A pounding in the distance grew closer and louder—another explosion. There was little time to take cover. Debris fell everywhere.

'We are at war!' he thought. 'Could it possibly be true? It's the only plausible explanation!'

He saw twenty or thirty people nearby. Some were babies crying, either scared from the blasts or the daily routine of growing up. It didn't matter. It was chaos. He stood up and brushed off the dirt from his clothes.

Feeling dizzy, he reached his hand to his head and felt warm blood caking in his hair and oozing from a laceration.

Two medics saw him and walked over to help. One cleaned his head wound and wrapped gauze around his light brown hair.

The other gave him a large wipe to cleanse his bloody face where it had trickled down. They checked his vitals, searching for any signs of a concussion.

"School buses are coming to evac everyone out of the hot zone." said one medic.

"You should get on the next bus and go to the high school. The infirmary can tend to those wounds and stop the bleeding and possible infection."

A few minutes later, a school bus stopped in front of David and opened the door. A military issue gas mask hid the driver's features. His stringy black hair escaped between its straps.

"Hey, are you getting on the bus?"

"No, I'm ok. I think I'll hang back for a while and wait for the next bus. There could be others who need help."

"Don't wait too long; it's getting dark. Rumor has it, wild and domestic animals are looking for food! Not so safe at night. I think the last bus is at sunset."

"I'll be careful. By the way, why are you wearing a respirator, and civilian personnel aren't wearing any?"

The driver did not respond but closed the door and drove away.

David found a few more stragglers and walked with them to the high school, where the bus took the others. As the survivors stepped off the bus onto the sidewalk, they could smell fresh coffee, roast beef, and anything else one could want to eat. Empty stomachs and hungry babies compelled the crowd to move forward through the school gates. He stood there.

###

David heard a voice speak to him. He turned around and didn't see anyone.

"Who's there?"

"Do not be afraid, David, I am an angel of God bringing you a message! Do not go in! If you do, you will never come out!"

"What can I do? I have had no food, little water, no shower, or clean clothes." He did not know how long he had been unconscious or even if any of it was real.

"Be at peace. Our heavenly Father wanted me to warn you. At night, the administration will lock the doors, and the food is filled with a drug to help everyone believe the many lies.

All the clothing has GPS markers, and soon they will be able to eavesdrop on conversations."

"Okay! I won't go in." Then he was reminded of Esau's story of how he traded his birthright for a bowl of soup.

"Is it that serious?"

"Yes! The end is near, and God's church will soon be taken home by the Holy Spirit. Then the man of lawlessness appears. Many events have not taken place yet, and it will get much worse before the final shofar is sounded: "The Almighty God is calling His children home."

David noticed the large black letters mounted on the school's front: N.W.O. He remembered that a man approached his firm a year earlier to draw up plans to retrofit public schools. His business card read: New Wealth Organization.

He felt sick to his stomach and told the man he was too busy to take on another project at that time.

"Was that you?" he asked the angel.

"Father moved you in your spirit so that you would have nothing to do with them."

David felt nauseated again, realizing the dark forces terrible plans were advancing on a world that's asleep. He was thankful that God prevented him from taking that project.

David could not believe what he was seeing. The ruins, the chaos, and the total devastation were indescribable, and it wouldn't be long before news reached his brother John.

‘He’s going to be angry for me taking this job. Then he will be terrified.’ David thought.

‘Either way, I am in for a never-ending lecture.’

###

He stood at the entrance as buses were unloading passengers from the community, where Doc and his family lived.

Doc, his wife, and two kids climbed off the bus and brushed by David. In pain, tired, and hungry, he ushered his family through the gate, not knowing what to expect.

A bullhorn blared across the school grounds startled David back to the others' fear.

Chapter 2: *War Room*

The sign read:

PROPERTY OF N.W.O

AND AFFILIATES! NO TRESPASSING! VIOLATERS WILL BE PROSECUTED!

In the first week of February 2019, construction began at the old high school. The New World Order changed the name with large black letters N.W.O was now the old school's name. Most locals joked about the acronym's possible meaning, but no one came close; no one except believers who lived nearby.

On March 15th, construction workers arrived at the school. Trucks with drywall, plumbing supplies, and electronics entered the football field's main gate. Classrooms were being transformed into apartments for families, with bathrooms, showers, bedrooms, and closets, but curiously, no kitchens.

The doors were replaced by sliding doors with electric sensors, operating them in every unit. Tinted windows did not allow outsiders to see inside.

The workers were often stopped by community members and asked what was going on inside, but none gave up any information. Residents were getting worried and wondered why all the secrecy.

Trucks with khaki-colored uniforms arrived with specific sizes and numbers. The names of families secretly were already predetermined. Every uniform had GPS markers sewn into them.

Michael Adams, known as Doc, and his family are among the targets. He was unaware of the covert operation unfolding in his community. Like many others, Doc was having suspicions regarding the reasons behind the covert activities at the school.

Weeks went by while gardeners maintained the grounds. It appeared to be a routine ritual, mowing the grass, fertilizing the flowers and shrubs, and the general removal of clippings.

On April 11, 2019, there was a great disturbance. Satellite dishes lined the football field, and some stood on the roof of the main building. Sounds of scraping metal pierced the silence of the night.

Neighbors woke up from the screeching noises, heard for blocks. Flood lights directed at the school chased away the darkness. Workers were yelling orders to stage the operations safely.

The people in the community were furious! Cars pulled up at the school with drivers still in pajamas, yelling at the workers.

"We have to work tomorrow!" said one.

"Knock off the noise!" said another.

Their objections were unheard because of grating metal and the loud drone of motors from the cranes, trucks, and workers barking orders.

The residents agreed they would file an injunction against any more night work. Frustrated, they returned to their homes.

The school had no houses surrounding it. The plaintiffs would have difficulty demonstrating any disturbances in or around their neighborhood because the school was acres away from any homes. They felt they had to try.

###

The top floor of the high school converted into a war room. Ten miles outside of Albuquerque was a perfect location for the testing.

The school renovations housed the newest computer equipment. The satellite dishes were now in place and operational. A cell tower in the school field expanded the network's distance. Special signal scramblers were programmed to block outside communications to the area. Everything was moving forward as planned.

###

In the early twenty-first century, there was a big push for parents to allow their kids to attend school on their laptops at home. By 2017 most schools had closed, and the properties sold to private investors.

It saved the federal government billions of dollars in overhead and maintenance costs. The children were now taught in online classrooms with state-approved instructors and curriculum.

The religious schools, which remained open, were under attack by the government and mass media. Private Christian organizations did not receive government funding.

New World Order members had purchased most of the public schools, which housed surveillance equipment, satellite dishes, and the eight-foot cyclone fence created a formidable barrier.

The high school David stood in front of was no different. The high fences, the razor wire on at the top, and the guards patrolling made the school appear like a prison.

The lawns and fields were still clipped every week, which puzzled the communities, until the bombs started exploding. When the satellite dishes moved in, there was little doubt that some thought America was at war. Were these schools to become internment camps for Christians?

Behind a six-foot rosewood desk sat a man watching the latest broadcast. His black hair slowly surrendering to gray matched his silver glasses, which bounced back the television images.

"Is everything in place?" Sims asked.

"Almost sir. The test bombs exploded in old artillery ammunition dumps. The mechanics posing as power company employees accessed all the target homes and placed exploding devices in their basements, and none suspected a thing.

Giving the school children the chip test will be initiated on April 19th. No one knows about the biomedical chips, which will dissolve within ten to fifteen days.

The trial run is almost too easy. Isn't it amazing how simple it is to deceive 'sheep without a Shepherd,' so to speak?" Grayson laughed.

###

"It's not so much the deception, Tim, but the fears of who will provide their basic needs such as food, water, clothing, and a roof over their heads, which is exactly what the cult leader Jim Jones did."

Tim nodded, listening intently to his mentor.

"You know, Timothy, Jones ran multiple dry runs for suicide by drinking the juice without cyanide in it. He moved the church to Guyana and took everyone's passports.

Jones even switched husbands and wives which was another form of control."

"Are people that stupid? I wouldn't have left everything behind to follow that psycho!"

"Most people would not have followed him either. But, by the time the move was complete, he had already systematically created a codependence in his followers. The liquid testing ran for months until Jones had total control.

Anyway, Jim Jones' followers became used to the routine. When the day finally arrived for mass suicide, it was too late to back out.

Many ran into the woods, but Jones had stationed men with machine guns to kill anyone who tried to escape. Over nine hundred people died that day. Few escaped telling about it." said Sims.

He lit a cigarette and leaned back in his chair. Sims' demon thought how stupid humans are and reveled in controlling such an evil man. Isaiah Sims was so arrogant; he was easy to enter and possess.

'Spirit guide!' The demon thought and laughed, making Sims laugh. The demon controlled its host, even telling it what to say.

###

The atrocities of the twentieth century were precursors to the events unfolding. The destroyer was on the move seeking new victims, and the church had fallen asleep.

Anti-Semitism led to the holocaust, and over six million Jews died along with Italians and Russians. It was all in the name of Eugenics-racial purity- which failed.

But they would not return to the homeland of their ancestors until 1947.

The British relinquished their claim, and President Harry Truman, along with the United Nations, declared Israel a sovereign nation in 1948. Israel was recognized internationally as an independent state. God's people had returned to the land of their birth.

###

America celebrated Israel's independence, and the destroyer moved onto the United States. One by one, freedoms were systematically removed. First, it was prayer in school. Later, abortion -the murder of unborn babies- was allowed. Babies can now die on demand, even at birth.

The State of New York passed a law that gives a patient and doctor the latitude to allow a delivered child to die. The stripping away of American liberties has been both insidious and sinister.

In the twenty-first century, anyone quoting scripture to gays is now a hate crime. The enemy has used young teens to execute mass murders of school children. The right to bear arms is now in jeopardy. God's church is still asleep, but will it wake up before it is too late? Only God knows.

Chapter 3: *Fear*

Stress is high. It is always a busy time for Dr. John Garner. Tax time also increased the visits from pre-retired patients. Anxiety levels were higher, which often manifested the stress in physical ways. Insomnia, elevated blood pressure and change in appetite were just a few of the issues affecting seniors. John knew that tax time was stressful for everyone and tried his best to reassure his patients.

Julie, John's wife, also took great care in showing her paintings in her gallery located in Pioneer Square. It was common for her to spend extra time at the gallery arranging paintings, placing new ones on display, and promoting her latest show.

Tax time was different for her because her large sales stemmed from the influx of tax refunds. Many visit The Gallery, as both locals and tourists shop for a piece of memorabilia from a Seattle artist.

Julie's artwork was internationally known and recognized in the mainstream art community. She chose the Seattle skyline and landscapes of the Puget Sound, reflecting the beauty which Seattle has to offer. Ferry terminals with the backdrop of the Space Needle were the most popular. Patrons loved it.

In the early years as an artist, Julie offered weekend classes at Shoreline, Highline, and other junior colleges in the area. As opportunities increased, she began to focus on painting in her home studio. Eventually, she opened The Gallery and displayed her art.

The notoriety she received was overwhelming. Julie's gallery was featured in Art Today, a magazine devoted to discovering new talent. The magazine also ran the article on its social media website, and Julie's work went viral.

Now, in 2019, Julie has two galleries in the Seattle area. She limits interviews and speaking engagements so she can concentrate on painting. Her managers oversee the galleries well and occasionally lets her know regarding a large sale to a client.

She attends the sales, meeting with the client personally whether it is a hundred-thousand-dollar sale or five thousand; Julie humbly thanks the client in person for their support.

John is so proud of Julie and supports her in every way with her business. She has been his strength and soulmate for nineteen years. Julie helped John finish med school and raised their two children. The weekend classes enabled her to stay home.

It was 4:30 p.m. John's last patient had left the clinic. He went to his office and dictated the report into the recorder. He looked at his phone and saw that David had called.

He dialed David's number. It rang once, twice, and David answered on the third ring.

"Hey big brother, what's up."

Hey little brother, what's up with you? Are you ready to go to Albuquerque?"

Just about, I have to shop for some clothes because it is a lot warmer there than Seattle. Other than that, I'm ready."

There was an awkward silence. John thought the trip was a waste of time and did not want his brother to leave.

He was also feeling guilty for not seeing him more often since they live in the same city. He cleared his throat.

"John, are you okay?"

"I'm fine. Hey, do you want to come over for dinner tonight? You know, so we can visit before you make this big move?"

"Come on, John. It's not forever! It's only for a few weeks, maybe a couple of months at the most."

"Yeah. okay. About dinner, are we on?"

"Sure, what time?"

"See you around seven?"

"Okay, see you then."

John hung up, grabbed his medical bag, and headed out the door. The breeze rising from the Puget Sound brought a chilling bite in the air. The garage did little to block its attack. As he eased out of the garage, a light rainfall began, adding to the wet cold.

The congested freeway already had commuters racing to beat the rush hour traffic just minutes from emptying onto I-5. The express lanes were still open so John could avoid any tie-up.

He called Julie on his Bluetooth and told her David was coming to dinner. After he hung up, he took exit 171 off Interstate-5 and entered Green Lake Drive. Three turns, and he was home.

###

David parked next to John's BMW. His 2019 Subaru Outback was a beautiful Crystal White Pearl but paled next to John's car. The BMW is great for a doctor, but the Outback is perfect for an architect who needs to go on rough terrain. The all-wheel drive made the trips easy.

John was sitting in his brown leather Easy Boy recliner when the doorbell rang. He looked at his watch, which showed seven o'clock. David was always punctual. Katrina opened the door, and David walked in with Julie's bouquet.

"Always on time, David." John hugged him.

"David!" It's so good to see you!" Julie hugged and kissed him on the cheek.

"These are for you."

"Come in, Come in." Julie gave Katrina the flowers, and the three walked into the living room.

"So David, tell me about this General Casey guy."

"My firm was contacted back in February to see if I could help him renovate his hunting lodge in Albuquerque. I pulled together some preliminary drawings based on the photos he sent me. He liked what he saw and agreed to meet with me here in Seattle to go over them. Because of previous commitments with both of us, we met in March."

John sipped on his straight-up Scotch while listening to David. It all seemed suspicious to him.

'This guy from New Mexico calls him to draw up blueprints for his lodge, and he couldn't find anyone local? Curious.' He thought.

"John, are you listening?"

"Yeah, David, of course."

"Billy hung around for a few days after. It was great! He is a Christian, John!"

"Wonderful!" said John rhetorically.

Julie smacked his arm, and John got the message. 'Knock off the attitude,' was loud and clear as the slap echoed.

"Right, shall we eat?"

John fixed another drink. Julie and David preferred ice water with lemon slices. Beef Wellington with baked potatoes, steamed asparagus spears, and a small dinner salad was the evening meal.

After dinner, Katrina brought out hot fudge sundaes. John rolled his eyes in mock objection, and everyone laughed.

As the evening ended, David hugged John and told him that everything would be alright. John hugged him back.

"Don't worry, John; God has got my back. And yes, I will call you often, okay?"

"You'd better! I worry about you, you know."

"I know. I love you, brother."

"Good night David."

John worried about David all day, making it difficult to see patients without being distracted. He knew that David's flight landed at 2:41 p.m. in Albuquerque. He finally said goodnight to work and left. John's phone rang.

"This is Dr. Garner."

"Well, hello, Dr. Garner."

"David! I was just about to call you."

"I figured. A limo picked me up and brought me to my apartment. John, it is amazing! Billy stocked it with food and even leased a car for me!"

"I'm glad to hear you're okay. So are you getting settled in?'

"I knew you would stew about me, big brother! But that's what big brothers do, right? And yes, I am settled in."

"You know I promised mom and dad..."

"I know, I know John, and you have kept your promise and then some."

"Just keeping tabs on you little brother."

"Mom and dad would be so proud of you. I am too."

"Thank you, John, that means a lot to me. Anyway, I'll call you tomorrow, okay?"

"You better." John laughed and hung up.

Telling David, he is proud of him is the closest he came to saying 'I love you' to David. Maybe he worried too much for his kid brother. Hearing the excitement in David's voice seems to reassure him that everything will be okay.

It was 2 p.m. in Seattle, and he was eagerly awaiting David to call. John had few appointments that day and was preparing to leave the office. Then he saw the news on the breakroom TV.

"This is KING 5 NEWS with a special news bulletin. "Today, April 18th at 1:30 p.m. in Albuquerque, New Mexico, multiple bombs exploded in and around the outlying areas! It is unknown the cause or how many casualties there are! Stay tuned to King 5 News Seattle, for new updates as they occur! We now return you to normal programming."

John Garner drove his silver BMW into his driveway on Green Lake and ran inside. His wife, Julie, thought he might have lost a patient as he specialized in elderly care.

"Are you okay, John?" she asked. "You seem so down today."

"Haven't you been watching the news?" he asked. "Bombs have been going off in the southwestern parts of the United States!"

"I'm sorry, I've been in the studio all day painting and listening to classical music." Julie replied. "Did the news say where?"

John was getting frustrated with her and poured himself a Scotch on the rocks. He tossed a large gulp to the back of his throat and swallowed hard.

'This is going to be a three Scotch night!' he thought and refilled his glass. Julie was getting worried and tried to help John calm down.

"Honey, please sit down and tell me what you heard."

"Julie, please." he replied and hesitated, clearing his throat.

"David went to Albuquerque, New Mexico, two days ago.

"Didn't you just talk to David a couple of nights ago?"

"The bombs are going off just outside of Albuquerque! That is where David's condo is!"

"Have you been able to reach David at all?" she asked, tearing up.

"No! There is a complete satellite and cellular blackout because of the military bomb specialists. Any type of frequencies could detonate the bombs while in transit, or so the media says!" He choked down the last of his drink.

Katrina stepped into the living room.

"Please excuse me. Dinner is ready!"

Julie took John's glass and refilled the ice pouring another Scotch and placed it at his spot on the dining table.

Dinner was silent. Julie knew not to interrupt John's thoughts when he was so upset. Half-eaten salad, ribeye steak, and buttered zucchini were cleared, and dessert was New York cheesecake garnished with strawberries and drizzled with chocolate fudge syrup. It was John's favorite.

He took his fork and sliced a small piece and ate it. The flavors of strawberries, chocolate, and the cheesecake catapulted John back to his childhood. He and David used to argue who got their favorite dessert.

"Mom," John yelled to the kitchen, "David said you made his favorite dessert and not mine! It's my turn to have my dessert tonight!"

"John?" said mom. "You are fifteen years old, and David is seven. Why do you have to bully your brother over something so small as dessert?"

John turned red. Mom brought David's sundaes to the table. John ate it anyway because it still tasted so good. Then dad spoke. John knew it was another 'Does this please Jesus?' speech.

"You know John, David is your little brother and wants to be your best friend. Jesus says it's okay to disagree, but not to the point of being mean."

'I wish I had listened more to you, dad.' He thought and mechanically drank the balance of his third drink.

Katrina reentered the living room with coffee. Chef Anna cleaned the kitchen before leaving, so Katrina would not have the whole task.

"Will there be anything else?"

"No, Katrina. And thank you, I apologize for being less gracious tonight. My brother…"

"Yes, sir, I know. I heard you tell Miss Julie. I called my husband, and we have already started a prayer chain for David."

"Thank you. David is going to need all the prayers he can get. We can clear away our coffee cups. You have a good evening and thank Jesse for the prayers."

John knew that Katrina's husband was a pastor of an evangelical church. He also remembered his dad saying that sometimes prayer is the only option.

'Maybe I can fly into the hot zone because I'm a doctor.' He thought. 'I'll check out the flights; since I have some time off, I can go and be back in three days.'

Frustrated by the current events unfolding, he walked down the hall to the den and pressed the button to his computer. The light flashed, and the electronic device came to life.

He knew Alaska Airlines flies there several times a week. John keyed in his personal information and searched for Albuquerque's flight in the early morning. The first flight was full—the second one, also full. Then the third and the fourth, all full.

"What is going on!" he said. "He slammed his hand down on his mahogany desk. Julie ran in.

"What is the matter? Are you okay? I heard a loud noise."

"I'm okay, and that was me smacking the desk. I'm angry because I decided to catch a flight to find David, and all the flights are full, booked, no room!"

"Honey, why don't you call the airline and book it over the phone. Maybe the application is not responding," she said and kissed his forehead.

His anger defused momentarily. He took Julie's hand and said, "That's why I married you, my dear because you are so smart." Then he kissed her hand. She smiled, and John picked up his cell phone.

"This is Alaska Airline. My name is Christy. How may I serve you today?"

"My name is Doctor John Garner, and I'd like to book a first-class flight to Albuquerque, New Mexico, as soon as possible." There was silence on the other end.

"Hello? Christy? Are you there?" More silence.

"I'm sorry, sir, I am searching through the database, and it appears that all flights in or out of Albuquerque, New Mexico, have been canceled until further notice."

John jumped out of his chair, slamming it against the bookcase behind him. His face turned red and sweat began to form around his collar.

"I don't think you understand the level of urgency, Christy!" he said sternly. "Let me speak to your supervisor! Now!"

Chapter 4: *Old Billy*

As David pondered all these things; a man spoke up in the group.

"Hi, my name is old Billy."

"Right," the crowd chimed in, "the gun shop owner."

David made his way to the front of the crowd.

"Billy, am I glad to see you!"

"My house is only a few clicks from here. If we hurry, we can make it before dark." said Billy.

About twenty people followed at a hurried pace as Billy and David led the group. At the top of the hill, the town and school disappeared into the distance.

His confusion grew as he left the school, the angels, and the muffled whispers behind. The events at the school seemed too surreal to believe. David stopped and looked back.

Billy spoke of the cold war between the former Soviet Union and the United States.

"Hey! The people following us left."

"I guess none of them liked history in school. When I mentioned the cold war, they skedaddled." Billy smiled and put the key into the locked door to his gun shop.

"The animals are turning on each other. That part is true; I have seen it happen. I can't help but think that a chemical agent is being released into the air to affect the animals and make them more aggressive. I have my suspicions. Did you notice the bus drivers wearing Army issue respirators, David?"

"Yes, I did, and I asked a driver why he had one, and none of the civilian populous had any. He didn't reply but closed the door and drove away. I also know the brothers and sisters in Christ who are surrounding the school are safe." He did not elaborate.

Billy turned the dead bolt, and the two walked to the alarm panel.

"I also believe that God is protecting them from the chemical agents released into the air."

David noticed that weapons and ammunition were readily available to the public.

"Did the National Guard come to your shop and remove all the weapons from the secret armory?"

"They only thought they did, David. The military does not know about my second home.

"Second home?"

Billy smiled, turned the same key in the alarm case, and opened the control panel.

"Tracy, this is old Billy; please disengage the alarm system so that we can come home."

"I know what to do."

Billy waited; a gun shelf popped open, and they walked downstairs, passing a large vault on the left beside the hallway to the underground house. The immense steel framing on the wall incased the entire length of the underground structure.

"This is my armory. I've been building up my arsenal in case war broke out in our country. Since I became a Christian, I now rotate items I can sell to the public. I have no interest in killing anyone."

"Those with the mark of the beast no longer belong to God," David said.

"I know, but I have mixed feelings about killing anyone. As a General, I've had my share of killing and giving orders to kill.

During the Bay of Pigs, which happened during the late 1950s, I had a bomb shelter constructed. I placed a hunting lodge over the shelter and stocked it with military weapons and a few special ones if there was an incursion. The shelter is inside the vault.

Flash grenades temporally blinds an intruder, and the percussion of the blast would make anyone senseless and off-balance. It takes several minutes for the perpetrator to regain their senses, and by then, the perps are neutralized."

"How long did it take you to build this facility?"

"Approximately twenty years, give or take. I was still in the Marine Corps when 9/11 happened. I was a Brigadier General stationed at the White Sands military base.

On September 11, 2001, when terrorist attacks struck the two World Trade Center towers in New York City, I felt a sense of urgency. I wanted a safe place for the possibility of a Third World War. Since I was still in the military, it made it easier to get the research I needed." He said and sipped his coffee.

"The list of agencies was exhausting. I started with the Department of the Interior, which sent me to the Department of Defense, who sent me to Homeland Security. The side-skirting seemed endless.

Finally, I used one of my aides trained in government shenanigans 101, who knew how to circumvent all the proverbial buck passing, by name dropping -mainly mine- to get the answers I needed. The USGS-United States Geological Survey- was the most helpful."

"How long did the research take to complete?"

"You'd be surprised how quickly a General in the Marine Corps can get things done. Besides, there was no way of knowing if I would use the information to build a secret facility for the military or not. They had no clue it would be my secret facility. Hence military retiree and proud owner of Old Billy's Gun Shop. Since I was in Special Ops, the National Guard had no problem placing their ammunition cache in my shop. It made for a nice tidy extra income."

Billy placed the hunting lodge over the underground corridors and bomb shelter. It rested high on a knoll that gave old Billy a 360° view of the surrounding countryside.

The balcony windows were also computer screens, and the lodge had cameras and did the same sweep of the area every hour, projecting the images onto the windows.

It was all rock reinforced, and the basement has false corridors and dead ends in case someone from the lodge wandered downstairs.

###

There were bedrooms with baths on the main level, so family and friends could stay. A corridor led to six bedrooms in the basement, each having its hallway. All entrances begin in the common room, where the dining and meeting areas are.

There were seven corridors: six led to private rooms, and the seventh spilled out onto a secured balcony. The basement was the top of a more critical infrastructure that took more than fifteen years to construct.

General William Casey had been building six floors out of solid rock extending a hundred meters below the surface. It would later house countless Tribulation Saints during the last terrible seven years before Christ's return.

###

Two hundred solar panels supplied the electricity and warmth to the lodge, hot water tanks, and outbuildings and the six levels below their feet. Billy sold the extra electricity to the local electric company.

"I know you are hungry, David, but I thought you might like to shower and change into some clean clothes. I promise there are no GPS chips in your clothing." Both men laughed.

David moved to the first corridor and saw his name on a small brass name plate to the right of the entrance.

He chuckled and walked down the passage to his room. He stood in front of the door as it slid open.

The room revealed a cascade of color splashing into David's senses. A hint of red and orange kissed the browns, greens, tans, and yellow, beckoning David inside.

The private deck had a free-standing fire dish to the left. On the right were tan cushioned chairs hugging the Jade table where several desert flowers were centered in the natural fountain.

###

He opened the closet door and found a complete wardrobe in his size, taste, and styles. The dresser was laden with underwear, socks, and tee-shirts, all folded militarily.

The second drawer had several pairs of pajamas ranging in color and style.

The sink had electric and hand razors resting on top of the bathroom counter. Tracy also made sure that David had toothpaste, toothbrushes, and a drinking cup.

The central computer controls everything. Water in the sinks and the water jets overhead and down the sides of the shower.

It was 4 p.m., and the adrenaline David experienced earlier was wearing off. Fatigue and pain gripped him.

He undressed and saw his body with bruises and abrasions, looking more like a physical assault.

He stepped into the shower and closed the door. A voice came on.

"Please specify water temperature." Stunned, David said, "101◦."

The water began slowly with a fine mist. It increased to a spray, and David saw the caked-on mud and blood flow down his body. He slowly turned in the shower. The pain intensified by the water jets. Yet it also felt comforting.

David took shampoo and rubbed it into his hair. He grimaced from the soap touching the wound. The dried pasty blood flowed from his scalp down the drain.

The body wash was a soothing lavender and Aloe. He gingerly washed and allowed the final remnants of dirt to slide away.

"Water off."

"Please stand by for the sonic dryer."

A blast of warm air covered David's body. Air Jets slowly moved on David's skin, creating waves as the water surrendered to it and David's body felt the warm caress of the air drying him.

He stepped out of the shower, clean and dry, thankful he did not have to use a towel except for his hair and feet. He put on deodorant and cologne and brushed his teeth. Getting dressed was more brutal than he imagined.

It took David twenty minutes from beginning to end for his grooming, but feeling the bruises with every movement, it took him almost an hour. He slipped on a pair of sneakers and tied them.

'What a chore that was!' he thought.

He stood up and walked to the mirror to brush his hair. The wound on his head was sore but did not bleed. The rejuvenating shower and clean clothes on; he now focused on hunger.

There was a knock on the door, and it slid open.

"Well, David, what do you think?"

"It's amazing, but how did you know I would like this room?"

"David, you remember when I said I was well off? I came from old money and lots of it. I am an only child, so when my parents passed, I inherited all of it! Since I was a professional in the military, they had no problem making me their sole heir.

"With that said, I check out everything, even people that will enter my life. I hope that does not offend you, but being from Special Ops, a Marine must look at every contingency. The knowledge I have could put the entire country at risk."

"I'm not offended, but that still doesn't explain how you knew what I would like."

"It's simple. While you were in college, I learned a lot about you. One of your professors was so impressed with you that he talked about you all the time."

"Let me guess, you two were buddies in the Marines, right?"

"That's affirmative." They laughed.

"Dinner will be ready in twenty minutes, Billy," Tracy said on the com link.

"Hope you are hungry, David."

"I haven't eaten in three days, I think."

"Good. I'd hate all this food to go to waste."

They both walked down the corridor.

###

The common room walls had a numbered print of Jesus by a famous child prodigy. Two plaques, hand-tooled in brass, including the Ten Commandments and Psalms 23, were also mounted with recessed lighting over each one. Cherrywood enhanced the common room walls with a matching oblong dining table.

Tracy laid a white linen tablecloth onto the table.

The China was an elegant white with a gold rim raising its beauty from the linen it rested on.

The silverware had rose designs embossed with gold adorned handles.

Billy and David sat down at the table. Tracy brought in carafes of hot coffee freshly brewed with several naturally flavored creamers made from heavy cream. Both poured coffees. While old Billy liked black coffee, David poured the vanilla creamer into his cup. He enjoyed lots of creamer. Billy waited for David's comment as he sipped his coffee.

"This coffee is incredible! Private stock?"

"Years ago, I thought about what shortages besides the basic foods would be. So, I bought a few coffee bean plants and imported them, mostly from Columbia. Do you like it? I do have stronger."

David shook his head as he sipped the magnificent brew.

The double doors to the kitchen swung open, and Tracy and her husband Jeffery carried in platters of food and set them in the center of the table. Sliced prime rib surrounded by baby red potatoes was tonight's entrée. Baby carrots smothered in Amish butter filled the room with its sweet aroma.

Jeffery returned with the small dinner salads made of a fresh spring mix of spinach, romaine lettuce, and kale. Chopped zucchini, grape tomatoes, and sliced avocados layered the top with a sprinkling of white cheddar. The salad dressing was a homemade ranch.

Both took off their aprons, hung them on a hooks by the kitchen doors, joined Billy and David, and poured themselves coffee.

"Dinner is ready," said Jeffery.

"Shall we thank God for what he has provided?"

"Father God, we thank you for this meal you have given us. We also thank you for bringing David safely to us. Father, we ask that the other four will reach us safely. In Jesus' name, Amen. Let's eat."

The platters circled the table as each took a portion of the delectable choices.

"David, this is Tracy, whom you've already met, and her chef husband, Jeffery Campbell."

"Pleased to meet both of you. How did you meet, Billy?"

"While I was still General Casey, a colleague introduced me to Jeffery. He had just graduated from Culinary school, and my friend knew I was looking for a good chef for my home as soon as I retired.

We met outside the Officer's Mess," and I asked a few questions."

"Are you married?"

"Yes, sir, to the most wonderful woman I have ever met. Her name is Tracy."

"What experience do you have?"

"Right now, I work in the Officer's Mess."

"That food is exquisite! Okay, I'll hire both of you. I have plenty of room for you to live in my home also."

"What Billy did not tell you is that Jeffery and I are Christians. We prayed about the job, and God helped us lead old Billy and Shelley to Christ." Tracy smiled.

Billy was a little embarrassed, forgetting such an essential part of their meeting, but a toothy grin surfaced as he turned a little red in the face enhancing his white shoulder-length hair.

There was a peaceful silence as each member ate their dinner except David. He shoveled his food as fast as he could, not remembering the last time he had such a good meal.

He looked up, and the others were staring at him.

"What?" he asked. "I'm sorry, but my last meal was days ago, I think. Forgive my lack of manners."

"Compliments to the chef, I'd say." Jeffery laughed. "I hope you saved room for dessert."

"Indeed, I did." replied David realizing as he spoke how much his stomach had shrunk.

Tracy and Jeffery quickly cleared the dinner dishes and brought in chocolate mousse with sliced strawberries drizzled in white chocolate. David was thankful it was a light dessert.

"Tracy, David, and I are going to move to the sitting area. Could you…"

"I know General, Biscotti and coffee, "she said and winked. The two were quick to clean up and make the kitchen spotless.

Two new carafes of coffee and biscotti sat on the coffee table.

Billy nodded, and Tracy transferred the computer controls to the house over to him.

"Computer, finish the transfer."

"Identification required."

"Old Billy."

"Verification code."

"Toothy grin."

"Transfer completed."

"Tracy and Jeffery already have their computer codes. So will you, David. You will need to know all the codes for the alarm system and emergency protocols in case of an incursion.

"When do we start?"

"Tomorrow. I have a few things that we must do to secure the buildings. Then we can continue regarding the cold war discussion."

Billy keyed in codes to the security system, and all the compound locked down. Finished, Billy looked at David and continued his story.

"There are important elements that the president did not disclose. Do you remember the Cuban Missile Crisis in the sixties when John F. Kennedy was President?"

"I remember reading about it in school." David replied.

"The former Soviet Union leader, Nikita Khrushchev, had covertly placed several Nuclear warheads in Cuba 90 miles off Florida's coast.

For that time, they were high-tech intercontinental ballistic missiles, or ICBM's for short. 1,212 miles could place a rocket on the doorsteps to the White House and Congress, wiping out our entire political infrastructure within a matter of minutes.

No one knew that the U.S.A. had nukes in Turkey, right next to the former U.S.S.R.

President Kennedy made a deal with Khrushchev. If he removed the nuclear armaments out of Cuba; Kennedy, in turn, would remove the missiles out of Turkey. President Kennedy was more worried about Fidel Castro turning them on America. Vice President Lyndon Johnson was never informed.

J.F.K. knew about the nukes on October 16, 1961. He did not notify the American public until October 22, 1961.

President John F. Kennedy gave Khrushchev an ultimatum. Remove the nuclear weapons from Cuba, or a naval blockade would be initiated. That was the most volatile time in American history when the world came closest to a nuclear war."

"That is interesting, Billy, but what is the relevance today? We live in the year 2019, and the Cuban Missile Crisis happened some fifty-eight years ago."

"David, there are more Communist countries now than in the sixties and guess who is selling these countries nuclear capabilities; Vladimir Putin."

"You're talking about Iran and North Korea, right?"

"Those two countries are only the beginning, and it's not going to stop there. India also has nuclear armaments. Russia is just getting started. Vladimir Putin is working at restoring the former Soviet Union, and he doesn't care how.

"Ahh, Here comes the coffee and the chocolate almond Biscotti."

David embellished his coffee with the vanilla creamer that Jeffery made earlier.

Swirling the chocolate almond biscotti around in his coffee, he took a bite of the coffee-soaked cookie and allowed it to melt in his mouth. David could taste the dark chocolate meld with the almond titillating every taste buds.

Jeffery's biscotti was an epicurean experience. A sip of the vanilla-flavored coffee with the dark chocolate cookie remnant's taste was the crowning touch. After several minutes of coffee and biscotti, old Billy broke the silence.

"Jeffery, as always, your biscotti is exquisite. David, what did you think?"

"It wasn't coffee and biscotti; it was a journey into my pleasure center of the brain! My compliments to the chef!"

David raised his coffee cup to Jeffery. Jeffery blushed, Tracy agreed, and old Billy's laugh echoed down the bedroom corridors and spilling onto the balcony.

"You definitely have a way with words David. And Jeffery, you shouldn't be embarrassed either. God gave you your talent for cooking, so your gifts in the kitchen glorify Him every time you receive a compliment."

"You're right, Billy, but I have always had a hard time receiving praise from others."

"That's what makes Christians different. We are quick to give praises to others, but it is hard to receive praise. It is what keeps us humble because we know that the praise we receive belongs to God."

The evening surrendered to early morning as the four enjoyed reminiscing about college days, international cuisines, and personal testimonies for the love of Jesus. Tired from the day's stress before, everyone called it a night at 1 a.m. Tuesday morning. Billy had guests arriving at the lodge that morning, so he slept in his upstairs apartment. Tracy and Jeffery retired to their furnished apartment Billy built for them and placed it adjacent to the basement's lower level where the security facility and power grids operated.

David was the only one sleeping downstairs in the basement.

Tired, David remembered his condo destroyed and all his belongings. He went to the dresser, hoping, as he pulled open the second drawer.

'You don't miss a thing, do you, Lord.' David pulled out a new pair of light green pajamas. He looked for his Bible and realized it too was gone. Then David thought, 'Maybe,' and pulled open the bottom drawer and smiled. David found a brand-new Bible inside, with his name embossed in gold letters on the lower right corner.

There were also highlighters and red and blue pens lying on the writing desk. He fell asleep reading his new Bible.

Awakened by the aroma of fresh-brewed coffee, David walked out, still in his PJ's, into the common room where carafes of the steaming nectar were placed on the table with fresh creamers.

Tracy and Jeffery were already busy prepping for breakfast. Fresh cinnamon rolls emerged from the oven awaiting the cream cheese icing. David fingered through scripture as the aromatic fragrance of cinnamon teased his nose.

He could not remember the last time his mom had made such delectable pastries. She went home to be with the Lord a few years earlier, but he still missed her very much.

Tracy appeared from the kitchen and walked over to David.

"Good morning David. Did you sleep well?'

"I fell asleep reading my Bible. I'm still sore from yesterday."

"The cinnamon rolls aren't quite ready yet but will be ready to serve in about fifteen minutes or so. Since it is still early, Jeffery thought a late brunch might be a great change for this morning. The cinnamon rolls are just a teaser."

###

David read his morning paper with coffee, but he read his Bible since no newspaper was forthcoming.

Finishing his first cup of coffee, he poured and doctored another and headed back to his room to shower and get dressed.

The shower was both painful and comforting; unbearable because of his wounds and sore muscles, comforting relaxing the sore muscles. Dressing was a bit of a chore because the soreness preempted his typically agile movements, which he took for granted.

Drinking the last sip of coffee, David returned to the dining room where fresh coffee, creamers, and a large tray of cinnamon rolls adorned the table. He picked up the freshly glazed confection and put one on his saucer.

The coffee was so good that David poured himself another cup, though he often limited himself to two a day.

He sat sipping his coffee, politely waiting for everyone else to gather. Jeffery and Tracy hung their aprons and joined David at the table.

"You didn't have to wait for us to eat. Old Billy will join us for brunch because he is dining upstairs this morning with some Marine buddies; anyway, thank you for waiting.

"Last night, I was starving; this morning, my manners have returned." David laughed.

###

After he cleaned the kitchen, Jeffery began preparing the mid-morning brunch menu. Tracy placed a laptop in front of David while sitting on the sofa opposite the coffee table.

"Billy instructed me to start your training on the computer and learning the codes. You will have to know all our codes and yours as well.

There is a special code to be used only if an incursion happens. This code will automatically encrypt all other codes making it impossible to break."

"I did not realize there is so much to learn," David replied.

"Did you show him the virtual tour of the beds below us on the other six floors yet?" old Billy asked as he walked in.

"Beds? What beds? Floors? What floors?"

Chapter 5: *Chipped*

Sims lit a cigarette laced with cocaine. "You see, Grayson, the messiah, is a master of deception. He will be here soon, and we need at least three to four more bogus chip implants to assure the same results. People have already accepted the chips in their debit and credit cards."

"Do you think Lucifer will be pleased with our results?"

"That depends," Sims replied and took another draw off his cigarette and exhaled. "If we are dead, it won't matter."

The test section was in the United States' southwestern part. Areas like the Pacific Northwest and the eastern seaboard knew nothing about the test bombs or the covertly placed microchip implants.

For the rest of the country, it was the daily routine of husbands and wives going to work and returning home to dinner and the news.

Government spin was at its best. The news media had so many different twists on the truth; the best-written novel could not keep up. The media followed orders and kept spoon-feeding lies to the general public.

"Old WWI and WWII bombs were exploding at random in the southern and southwestern parts of the U.S. The army has deployed several bomb experts in the disposal regarding this critical matter. Dry ice is used to reduce the temperature of these explosive devices.

Reportedly these left-over bombs have corroded casings and are now excreting nitroglycerin-the main propellent. The desert is the best place to destroy them. The dry ice will make these receptacles safer to move as a precaution to the bomb specialists. A temporary black-out of satellite and cellular communications will be implemented during the blasting operations.

We will keep you apprised when it is safe for these services to resume, ANW T.V. reports."

"That should appease the east and west coast for a little while. Funny how people will believe anything, especially if it is in the form of a special news bulletin." The program producer laughed.

###

Again, David was dreaming; though confused, he allowed the dream to continue. Questions erupted in his consciousness, unable to separate the reality of what is real and what is false.

'The Holy Bible is a recording of what was, what is, and what is to come.' He thought. Was he having a conversation with the Holy Spirit or was Dementia and Alzheimer's, setting a trap so insidious that once caught, they eat away the mind? Then it is too late! No one sees it coming.

David thought about his age and the two vermin crouching near him like camouflaged leopards waiting to devour the rest of his life.

The Holy Spirit begins another dream or part of the same one.

"Be at peace." He said and took David away in the spirit.

"Where are we?"

"Just watch and be still."

"They can't see us, right?"

He looked at David with a silly expression.

“Okay, I know, dumb question.”

He smiled,

“I want you to hear and see everything; that is why I want you to be still.”

He kissed David on the forehead and then placed his index finger to his lips and whispered, “Quiet.”

David realized all the endless stories in the small leather book are correct, and his doubts vanished. He was in the presence of pure majesty.

He had so many questions to ask his teacher, but David’s thoughts were interrupted by His. “In due time, little one. Now listen.”

Their focus returned to the two men in the war room.

“You smoke, don’t you, Timothy? Go ahead, take one. These are the best on the market.”

“Thanks,” he replied and lit up a cigarette. “Wow! What is in these smokes? I feel a little, little off, or…”

“High?” Sims cut in. “Nice, aren’t they? The High Council decided to spice up the nicotine with different types of opiates. The addiction process will help all smokers to accept the master’s mark, or their license to smoke is revoked!”

“What a joke! You can’t smoke if your head is gone!”

“Don’t worry, Tim, our cigarettes have small doses. Ours are harmless except for a good laid-back feeling. It is not addicting and has been used for decades to treat terminal cancer patients suffering from chemotherapy's side effects. You know, Marijuana.”

“Why am I feeling sick?”

“Sorry, Tim, I should have told you to take one or two puffs. You got three times the amount for a nonsmoker of pot. Here, take this and get some rest. I will not need you anymore today.

It will be a long day tomorrow; and don’t drive on that stuff; you could get into a wreck.”

'Pharmaceuticals are a major player in the deception as well.' David thought. 'What do I do with this information, Lord?'

"In due time, little one. Trust me." said the Spirit, and David was back in his room smelling hot cinnamon rolls.

'Did I just dream that Billy said there are lower levels?'

Chapter 6: *Panicked*

Christy politely answered John.

"Sir, with all due respect, my supervisor will tell you the same thing."

"Put your supervisor on the phone now!"

"One moment, please." she said and placed John on hold.

"John, what's wrong?"

"All flights to and from Albuquerque are canceled until further notice! And Christy put me on ignore!"

"John, calm down! You're going to have a stroke! Your face is beet red, and you are sweating everywhere!"

"Yes, yes, I know! What?"

A voice came on the other end of the phone.

"Christy? No sir, my name is James, and I am the shift supervisor in booking. I am at the top of the chain of command. Christy told you what I had ordered all my agents."

"James, I am a doctor and want to get to Albuquerque so I can offer assistance there!"

"I understand your frustration, sir, but the FAA gave direct orders that all air space has been closed due to the bombs exploding.

The United States military gave the order about half an hour ago. Even the FAA's hands are tied."

John let out a forced sigh and allowed his anger to dissipate.

"Isn't there anything you can tell me that might help?"

"I have heard that the military will be asking for medical teams to volunteer to go where the bombs went off. It's still unofficial and the press has not received the release yet. I hope this helps, sir. And I hope you find your loved ones okay."

"Thank you, James. You've been a great help. Please tell Christy I am sorry. It wasn't personal."

"She knows, sir. You are not her first worried caller. Good luck." James said and hung up.

John had a friend he grew up with, a doctor stationed out at Joint Base Lewis McChord, Washington. He called him.

"Jason, how are you? It's John."

"I haven't talked to you in a couple of months. How's David doing?"

"That's why I'm calling Jason. David is in Albuquerque."

"Oh boy. How can I help, buddy."

"I need to get there to find David. All the airlines have canceled flights to and from Albuquerque until further notice. He's my only brother, man. I can volunteer as a doctor and be airlifted to the hot zone and offer my services on the ground."

"How did you know about that? I just received orders to go there! Hold the phone."

Jason put John on hold and spoke to his commander. What seemed to be endless silence was only five minutes when Jason came back.

"How soon can you get here, John?"

"Seriously? I can hire a helicopter and be there less than an hour!" he replied.

"We won't be deployed until 0600 out of McChord AFB next door to Fort Lewis. But the sooner you get here, the sooner you can be processed as a civilian personnel volunteer.

You could drive, you know." he replied and chuckled. He knew John's BMW was his baby, and he would never leave it on a military base.

"Hilarious, buddy. It would be much easier if you could get clearance for a commercial helicopter to land at Fort Lewis." he said and laughed.

"Are you kidding me?! Homeland Security is so tight it makes soldier's combat boots squeak! Excuse me, sir, are you the president or some kind of dignitary?!"

"Okay, okay, I know. There is an uncontrolled airport in Spanaway on the backside of Fort Lewis. You can pick me there. I'll call you when we touch down, and Jason, say hi to Katy for me, will you?"

"Will do. It is 1800 hours right now; what do you say we meet at 2000 hours. That gives you two hours to get your tail over here."

"Would you speak English for once in your life, please?" Then Jason said,

"That is six o'clock now, and you will touch down around eight o'clock. The big hand will be on the…"

"Okay, wise guy, see you at eight p.m., give or take," John replied and hung up.

He hurried out of the den and down the hall to the master bedroom. Julie was already packing his bag. She was so used to him volunteering worldwide; she knew what to pack. She gave him a big kiss and smiled.

"I've already called Jimmy, and he is on his way to Boeing Field and will meet you there in thirty minutes." she said and handed him his suitcase.

"I love you so much!" he said and kissed and hugged her.

"I didn't know if you wanted your computer, but your phone charger is in the bag. Have a safe trip, honey. Give my love to David." she said and walked him to his car.

John put his suitcase in the car and climbed into the driver's seat. He started the car and blew Julie a kiss, then back out of the driveway. Julie waved as he drove off.

Chapter 7: *Incursion*

"You already told me about the secret floors below us."

"David, I just came downstairs from the lodge. I am sure that I hadn't mentioned anything about the other…"

"Six floors below us?" David said, completing Billy's sentence.

"How?" Billy was dumbfounded.

"Last night, when I fell asleep reading my Bible, the Holy Spirit took me away in the spirit, and I was in the war room on the top floor of the high school.

Two men were talking about the bombs going off and how they had been strategically placed. Biomedical chips were also implanted in the people inside the school. I woke up and came out here to get some coffee.

Tracy said that we would have brunch and the cinnamon rolls were just a teaser. I went back to my room and showered.

When I came out, the cinnamon rolls were ready, and I put one on my plate and grabbed my coffee.

She also said you instructed her to teach me the security program and everyone's security codes and the emergency code.

If entered, it would make all other codes encrypted and unable to break. I mentioned that there was a lot to learn when you asked Tracy if she had shown me the virtual tour of the other six floors beneath our feet."

"David, this is the first time I have been downstairs since last night. Indeed, the Holy Spirit must have taken you away and returned you.

What is interesting is the fact that you were able to see the enemy's camp and learn what the enemy is planning!

"Wow! What a revelation! Thank you, God! The bombs aren't going off randomly but have exploded by the enemy at specific targets."

"What I don't understand is why there is no satellite or cell service. We cannot even receive simple radio waves or television broadcasts."

"It is clear, David. If the enemy wants a test run, he must remove all forms of communication for the test to seem real, right? Isolation has been an extremely effective brainwashing technique for centuries."

"Billy," said Tracy, "That still doesn't explain what the rest of the U.S. is seeing, or globally for that matter."

"The powers of darkness have been working at deceiving everyone. As old, secret stockpiled bombs left over from World War I and World War II, the world sees a different crisis.

###

The bombs corrode over time and leach out droplets of nitroglycerin-which is the main propellant used in detonation-making the warheads highly volatile.

We see it as a war taking place because we are directly involved in the explosions, and all communications have abruptly stopped."

"That is why there is looting and panic. The people here, see the United States without a leader and hope. Billy, I get why the Holy Spirit showed me what is happening.

These events are a precursor to the rapture and the seven-year tribulation!

If this is a dry run, how many more will occur before the rapture, and how can we tell everyone directly affected by these events that they are not true?"

"That is an excellent question, David. Anyone who knows the truth and shares it right now is in danger! We have to be careful."

"Sorry to interrupt Billy, I heard most of the conversation and agree that we need to be careful, but we also need to be bold in our conviction." said Jeffery.

"I think that we need to be praying that God will bring those who think they are Christians to us so they can learn the truth."

"With that said, I need my wife in the kitchen for the rest of the prep work."

'Right." said Tracy and walked with Jeffery back into the kitchen.

Billy poured himself a cup of coffee and settled into a brown overstuffed chair directly across from David. The two sat quietly, each nursing their coffees.

Lights flashed, and an alarm sounded.

"David, stick close; you don't have your codes yet."

Billy handed David night vision goggles and a respirator. Tracy and Jeffery bolted through the kitchen doors, headgear in place, carrying automatic weapons.

They passed Billy and David their weapons, and the four proceeded to search the sanctuary.

A shadow moved in and out of the corridors. The computer squawked on. "There has been an incursion! Emergency protocols activated."

"Plug your ears!" Billy yelled.

A high-pitched frequency screamed throughout the complex. The shadow dropped.

"Perpetrator has been neutralized. Emergency protocols disengaged." said the computer.

The metal coverings on the windows retreated, and the lights returned to white. The four removed their goggles and respirators and clicked their weapons on safety.

Billy moved cautiously toward the stranger.

The infiltrator lay helpless in a fetal position on the corridor's floor, leading to the common room. The dizziness slowly left the man, and his six-foot frame stretched out. Billy smiled and gave a hand to him.

"It's good to see you, Jerry, but you weren't due until next week. What's the big idea of staging an incursion?"

"Well, since I created the system, I thought…"

"You thought you'd test it out, right? Everyone this is Jerry Roberts, our computer geek who is responsible for our entire security systems and scaring the daylights out of us."

The rest acknowledged him and put away the weapons and survival equipment. Tracy and Jeffery returned to the kitchen and finished prepping brunch.

David shook as he went back to his seat and sat down in front of the computer and his cold cup of coffee. Jerry poured a coffee and sat down next to David.

Tracy entered the room a few minutes later.

"Brunch is served," she said as if nothing earlier had occurred.

"Now, what about those six levels below our feet?" asked David.

Chapter 8: *Name*

"Ladies and gentlemen, please proceed to the gymnasium at 8:00 a.m. There may not be room for everyone, but don't worry, several large rooms have seventy-inch smart televisions that will accommodate all so that you can see and meet the prophet Isaiah Sims. Daycare is available for those who need it. Please utilize the daycare as Mr. Sims would rather there be no distractions by the little ones. Thank you."

The squeaking, clacking, and shuffling of shoes echoed in the hallways to the gym and the overflow rooms as they filled up. The excitement grew for the chance to meet the prophet.

None of the parents knew their children received microchip implants.

The rooms were full, and Timothy Grayson appeared on stage. He quickly hushed the room.

"The prophet's limo has been diverted from the area. An hour ago, anthrax appeared in the air and around the school!

Please stay calm, the CDC is here to help. Those in yellow survival suits will escort you to the emergency room set up out back in the football field in a few minutes. The CDC workers will inoculate you."

"Thanks to the messiah, the prophet barely escaped the deadly virus. Mr. Sims is allergic to the antidote and would have surely died."

The crowd shuffled through the double doors that led outside to the football field. Timothy exited the outside door behind the stage, lit a cigarette, and climbed into the limousine where Sims was waiting for him.

"Prophet, huh? Nice touch, Tim," he said and lit his smoke.

"Well, sir, I made it sound like the Pope was coming to town."

"Somehow, I knew I made the right choice when I recruited you. Tim, you are my right-hand man now."

"I'm honored, sir."

"From now on, no more sir stuff; it's Isaiah to you, okay?"

"Yes, sir, I mean, Isaiah."

The injection was on the top of their right hand. The CDC placed biomedical chips without their knowledge. The people would soon know and make the ultimate choice to either accept Jesus or renounce Him to receive the (chip) mark. It is a critical choice that will seal their eternal fate.

###

Lunch was served in the school. Everyone was standing in line to pick up their lunch. French dip sandwiches, French fries, salad, cakes, pies and ice cream, coffee, soda pop, and juices were all laced with chemicals to keep them hungry.

No one knew those evil people performed a dry run for the slaughter on those inside the school.

After lunch, the test subjects returned to their apartments and fell asleep. While they slept, a sedative gas seeped into the rooms. Nitrous oxide was harmless in small amounts but could kill in larger doses. The gas was also a test. But not everyone went back to their housing after lunch.

Some went outside to see what was going on. Christians were gathered in small groups, praying for those inside the fence.

"Father God," one pastor began, "We come before you at the throne of grace and ask you to open the eyes of the people who have gone inside the school.

Father, let them know they are being lied to and what is happening is not what is real."

Michael Adams, nicknamed Doc, approached the fence.

"What do you mean a lie!? They even inoculated us against the recent anthrax attack.

The injection was in the right hand. See, all of you outside the fence are going to die a horrible death unless you receive the injection too."

The pastor looked at Doc's hand and saw the lump about the size of a grain of rice. Pastor Ramone's color drained from his face.

"Young man, injections for diseases are never given in the hand to remove the threat of disease, especially the right one! I know this to be true because my wife is a doctor."

"You are wrong; the Center for Disease Control, aka, the CDC, came and injected all of us."

"Did you see any CDC vehicles in or around the perimeter of the school?"

"Well, no, but there were people inside with yellow survival suits on, and they took us to the emergency tents set up in the football field so we would be safe."

"May I ask you a question?"

"Sure, shoot."

"Have you ever gone to church?"

"When we were kids, my parents forced us to go. What has that got to do with anything?"

"So, you do know about Jesus and…"

"You know what I learned? It is simple! If you like Jesus, you are a good guy. If you do not like him, you're a bad guy!"

"There's more to it than that," replied Pastor Ramone as a national guardsman approached.

The camo gear and the AR-15 rifle were an intimidating presence at the high school grounds. The soldier walked over to Doc inside the fence perimeter.

"You need to go inside. Marshal Law has been initiated, and no one is allowed outside the billets."

"Wait a minute! I thought you guys were here to protect us from the animals; which ones, the four-legged or the two-legged?" Doc was visibly irritated by the soldier's insistence.

"Move along!"

The guard turned to the pastor and said, "You would be smart to keep your fairy tales to yourself!"

Doc slowly walked back inside, pondering everything the pastor and the soldier said. Something was not right, and he was going to get to the truth.

Chapter 9: *Helicopter*

John pulled into the parking lot at Boeing Field and paid for private parking in the garage for a week since he did not know how long he would be gone.

Grabbing his suitcase, John made his way downstairs and walked out onto the tarmac where Jimmy and his helicopter were. Jimmy was just finishing up his pre-flight check when John walked up. He had already filed a flight plan and gassed up the copter.

"Hey John, what's the urgency that you needed to fly out tonight to Fort Lewis?" He climbed into the pilot's seat inside the helicopter's clear bubble.

"David is missing." He climbed inside, putting on his headphones.

"He left for Albuquerque two days ago, and that's where the bombs are exploding."

"Sorry John, but why Fort Lewis? Why not book a flight directly?"

"I tried. The air space in and around Albuquerque is closed until further notice."

"Again, why Fort Lewis?"

"Jason Roberts is stationed there and has received orders for deployment to New Mexico. So, he cleared it with his commander for me to tag along. They need all the doctors they can get, and I can actively search for David."

"I can't touch down inside of Fort Lewis, but I can land in Spanaway. Is that close enough?"

"I know. That's where Jason agreed to meet me."

Jimmy cranked up the engine, and the rotors slowly moved. It took three minutes for the blades to rotate to flight speed. Cleared by the tower, they took to the air and headed toward Tacoma and Spanaway airfield.

The copter banked slightly to the left as Jimmy entered the prescribed vector approved by the flight tower.

The thirty-two-minute flight would have taken John two hours on I-5 from Seattle to Fort Lewis, especially since there is so much traffic, and I-5 was often a parking lot rather than an interstate freeway.

It was a beautiful night to fly. John paid no attention. At night, the Seattle bay is lit by city lights and the Space Needle shining in her splendor.

Flanked by ferry boats moving in and out of their Seattle terminals, the copter left the fluorescent city.

Tacoma bay was more silhouetted by industrial factories hugging the shoreline, and the starry sky was more visible. The copter moved inland and sped toward the uncontrolled airfield in Spanaway.

Jimmy touched down on the tarmac, and he and John said good-bye. When John was clear, Jimmy lifted off and flew the same vector back to Seattle.

Turning his phone on, John walked over to the asphalt driveway next to the airfield. His phone chirped and Jason was on the other end.

"Hi John, I thought you might be arriving earlier since Julie called me and told me that Jimmy was flying you here. So, buddy, I'm about three minutes out from the airfield. It's 7:05 p.m."

"Got it, I just walked from the tarmac, and I'm at the entrance of the driveway. See you in a few."

The apprehension John felt earlier returned and his memories slid back to their childhood.

"You know you're adopted, David, right?" John said with a sadistic grin for a sibling to torment the other.

David screamed, running to mom. "I'm not adopted!" He cried.

"John Robert Garner!" she yelled, "Get in here right now!"

Great, the little brat got me in trouble again.' He thought as he entered the living room.

"How could you even think of telling your brother something so mean when you know it's not true?"

"Come on, mom, he doesn't look like you, dad, or me; he has blue eyes and light hair. The rest of us have dark hair and brown eyes."

"I have told you before that he took after grandma and grandpa, who both had blue eyes and fair hair!"

John's guilt physically manifested in his eyes as tears formed. 'Sorry, brother.' He thought. 'I wasn't nice to you, was I, kid.'

A horn beeped, and a blue Mercedes pulled up to John. Jason pulled the car over and released the trunk latch.

Chapter 10: *Secret Home*

So, tell me, Billy, What's new?" Jerry asked, sipping his evening coffee.

Billy smiled, knowing that Jerry was taunting him to divulge his newest secret project. The onset of nightfall brought on a new sense of urgency for the small but growing team.

"First, let's go out to the main deck out back."

They walked over to the one-way glass that enclosed the balcony's entire length. In the daytime, the lodge relinquished the hills' reflection into radiant splendor. At night, the glass revealed only the darkness of the night to any outside onlookers. No one could see past the windows to the interior. It was completely private.

The computer cameras engaged an autorotation. The cameras surveilled the area every two hours and completed a 360° sweep of the perimeter. Superior night vision surveillance alerted animals large or small and any human activity, but only recorded human movement and old Billy loved to tinker and was always looking to improve what the military considered state-of-the-art devices. When he retired, he decided to keep his more recent developments to himself and his late wife, Shelley.

Before she passed away from cancer two years earlier, the two would sit for hours brainstorming, trying to develop new ideas that would make their dream home not only majestic but also impregnable to intruders. One instance would prove prudent to keep quiet.

###

"Tracy, please set the terrace open. We'll have our coffee outside tonight. Oh! See if there are any old-fashioned oatmeal-raisin cookies or some kind of cookie treats."

"Okay, Billy."

Tracy was always one step ahead of him. Coffee carafes sat on the table. Jeffery and Tracy reappeared from the kitchen with a tray loaded with homemade cookies, oatmeal-raisin, chocolate chip, and Vienna fingers filled with chocolate ganache. Everyone took a sample of their favorite cookies and refreshed their coffees.

###

The night lights were on, and the balcony camera rotation began at dusk. The giant green Saguaro cactus naturally surrounded the second secret home. As the desert surrendered to night, nocturnal animals were already on the prowl for dinner. Billy and Shelley spent countless hours on the balcony relaxing with the evening spectacles before she went home to heaven.

"Billy, I helped you with the night vision on these windows, but how did you get it to display like it was daylight?"

"You got rid of the greenish residue that has plagued the military for years."

"Shelley and I were working on it. As you know, she was an accomplished artist. So, we got to brainstorming about the essence of light. An artist knows that there can be no color in the absence of light.

We had to tweak it several times and finally asked God to show us, and "Viola," we did it."

"Okay, so you are saying that not only did you not sell this latest breakthrough to the government, but you also haven't filed a patent either? Why not?"

"It's simple. We live in the end times. The United States government will carry-out a sinister agenda-A.K.A.- the devil's. The dark forces inside our government focus on one thing, total control of America! We are the cornerstone of world democracy.

If the United States of America ceases to be a democratic republic with all the freedoms our brave men and women fought for, global freedom will also die!

It is not going to stop there. The elitists, those who are the world's most influential and wealthy, have signed their allegiance to dark forces.

The power brokers are manipulating world economies and fortunes. Since the tower of Babel, humankind has still had

a one-world ideology bent on global control. Its mastermind is Satan!"

"Well, this new technology will keep your secret home safe before an incursion can occur." said Jerry and laughed.

"You're right and the real secret are the six floors below us."

Chapter 11: *Executive Order*

"Grayson! Get in here!" yelled Sims.

"What's up, boss? I mean, Isaiah."

Sims trembled after reading the private memo sent to him through secret channels. The information he received could set back the next series of dry runs of bombings and chip implants.

'I don't get it.' He thought. 'Everything was operating so smoothly, and now this happens.' He lit a smoke and took a heavy drag.

"Tim, we have a major problem. Here read this memo."

"Today, the United States government has issued an executive order. All civilian agencies-private and government shall adhere to the guidelines outlined in this document:

- Assist all military and civilian physicians in administering medical care to those injured.
- Shall help in relocating those who lost their homes from the explosions.
- Institutions not limited to churches, private organizations such as charities and other private entities, and commercial concerns such as restaurants, hotel/motel services, and local government shall assist in the said needs in and around Albuquerque, New Mexico.

"I don't get it."

"It's simple, Tim. The good old U.S.A. has declared New Mexico a national disaster. It means that the controlled experiments we are handling, will have to be aborted for our security!"

Sims stared out the window across from his desk. His face turned red as he contemplated a possible breach regarding the secret society to which he belonged. 'If news gets out that we are not at war, we are dead men. Too many outsiders snooping around could ruin everything.' He thought.

"Can't we quietly reverse the food agents and stop the gas lines? Anyway, the chip will soon be gone and without a trace."

Tim walked to the window, turned, and leaned against it, waiting for Sim's reply.

"It takes several days for the agents to disappear from the bloodstream. The military and civilian populous are already on the way here.

When the people find out that there was no anthrax and the immunizations were bogus, there are going to be a lot of extremely angry individuals."

"Have you heard from headquarters yet? They probably already know about the orders."

The landline on Sims desk chirped, and Sims motioned for Grayson to leave the room. The phone was for the upper member's High Council to reach him securely.

Cell phones were too easily compromised. Isaiah Sims picked up the receiver.

"Yes, sir? Do you want explosive charges placed in the basement of the school? Yes, sir, I understand." Replacing the phone in its cradle. Sims buzzed Tim on the intercom.

"Tim, call in some bomb specialists within our organization to set charges inside the high school basement. Make sure that there are at least two world war II bombs moved into position as well."

"You're joking, right? There are over three hundred people inside the school, not to mention our staff. The High Council can't be serious, can they?"

"Do you understand the consequences if the public finds out? Our plan for the New World Order could be delayed by years, even decades! Just get it done!"

"Yes, sir," Tim replied.

He wondered how he could have bought into such an evil philosophy so insidious that they could destroy an entire community, especially women and children.

"Tim, this is the only way we can hide our tracks. Destroy the proof and run away. No loose ends. If we don't do this, you and I are dead men. The High Council will see to that!"

"I know Isaiah, but could this order be a little premature? I mean, the military isn't here yet."

"Unless an actual natural disaster happens, we will augment the plan of the High Council.

"Now my friend, make ready for Operation Boom."

Chapter 12: *Jason's*

John lifted his bag and placed it in the trunk. Jason climbed out and walked around the back, and hugged John.

"It's good to see you, old friend. I wish it were under different circumstances."

"As do I."

"Whoa, why so formal? You don't have to do that with me, buddy. However, it is a good idea though, when you address my superiors formally, at least until you get to know them."

Jason drove out to highway 7 and, turning right headed toward the back road that side skirted Fort Lewis. Highway 7 to the left led to Chrystal Mountain.

"You're right. Not knowing anything about David has got me worried."

"Well, we'll sort it out."

He pulled up to the guard shack at the front entrance.

"I have officer tags on my vehicle, but since you are a civilian, we'll have to go to the guardhouse and get you signed in."

"Sounds good."

Inside the guard center, the military guard snapped to attention and saluted Jason because he was still wearing his uniform. Jason forgot but obliged the soldier and saluted back.

Since 9/11, the heightened security required John's luggage be inspected. Satisfied that Doctor John Garner was not hiding a bomb in his bag, the soldier handed John a visitor's pass, and the two left.

"I forget about my uniform and have to salute those who salute me. I also am required to salute those higher in rank than myself. We'll meet the others at Madigan Army Medical Center in the briefing room."

Jason turned the key, sped away from the guard center, and drove toward his base housing.

A short skinny redhead with piercing blue eyes met them at the door. "John how are you?" asked Katie as she kissed his right cheek. John smiled and returned the peck on hers.

"How is Julie doing and the kids?"

"Julie is also worried about David. Jeremy and Kathy are both attending the University of Washington two years apart. Both try to come home when time allows."

"Since you two are getting up at O dark-thirty, I made a bed on the sofa for you, John. Also, I grabbed a pair of pajamas for you out of the guest room where Jason keeps extras.

There are also new toothbrushes in the bathroom. Good night." said Katie and hugged her two favorite guys and went to bed.

The two men went over the itinerary and their scheduled flight time. Jason gave John a badge that read 'volunteer' on it and a vest with a white medical cross on it.

An hour later, Jason went to bed, leaving John sitting in his borrowed PJs on the sofa. It was 11 p.m., and John's mind was too active to catch any sleep.

The scheduled flight time was at 6 a.m., and he laid down, trying to keep his eyes closed. The thought of losing his little brother was unbearable. Hundreds of 'what if' scenarios flooded his mind, chasing away any prospects of slumber.

The 4 a.m. alarm went off, and John's sleep-deprived mind and body mechanically moved to a sitting position.

Jason was already up and dressed in green chamoe fatigues with the pant cuffs bloused in with elastic ties-like miniature bungee cords- just above his boots.

Captain Roberts plugged a coffee pod into his coffee pot. Katie had Jason's TA-50 layout already inside the duffle bag, and Jason set it by the front door.

"Honey, I don't think I am going to need my entrenching tool-a collapsible shovel-this trip," said Jason and smiled.

"You never know what you'll need till you get there. Your mess kit is also inside."

John grabbed a quick ten-minute shower, brushed his hair and teeth, but did not shave. He dressed and entered the kitchen where his pod was brewing. Katie and Jason sat at the kitchen table drinking their coffees.

There was silence as John doctored his coffee with creamer and joined them. He cupped his coffee in his hands as he took his first sip contemplating the unknown future.

"John, I made reservations at the Officer's Mess for us to eat breakfast. The commander and his staff will also learn which protocols we'll use.

I know all this is going to be tough for you, but you will have time to search for your brother."

Jason kissed Katie goodbye, and the two went to the car. He deposited his duffle bag and John's suitcase in the back seat. Five minutes later, they arrived at the Officer's Mess.

There were salutes and handshakes. The officers seated themselves, with Jason's commanding officer sitting at the table's head. Over a dozen officers ranking from First Lieutenant to Colonel were present. Breakfast finished quickly, and Colonel Baker began the briefing.

###

"You have all been handpicked-some by invitation- to embark on a search and rescue mission. The difference, gentlemen, is this mission is on American soil. No one knows who the enemy is or what it will entail. Be on your guard!

What the press is releasing and what is happening could be inflammatory. Therefore, do not eat or drink anything offered to you other than by your fellow subordinates; is that clear?

Not even the National Guard is exempt from suspicion. They could be collateral damage. Doing what they are ordered and not knowing themselves, they are victims. Any questions?"

"Sir, does the government think this is a covert staging for WWIII?"

"At this point, Captain Roberts, I don't believe that the higher ups are dismissing any contingency. It could be that the old arsenal of bombs is detonating. But I do not think that it's random, and neither does the Pentagon.

I have authorized a press release for volunteers with medical backgrounds to accompany the military to find, save, and extract the injured as quickly as possible.

With that said, our first volunteer Doctor John Garner, offered his services to aid in this crisis. Your friend Captain Roberts explained that your brother David is among the missing."

"Yes, sir, he was transferred two days ago to Albuquerque, New Mexico, to design a multi-million-dollar facility for a retired General William Casey. The last time I heard from David was the night before last."

"Interesting! General Casey and I go way back. I will make sure that you have time and personnel to look for your brother and the General.

Gentlemen, There is a bus waiting for us at the 425th Welcoming Center to transport us to McChord Air Force Base. Dismissed."

More salutes and handshakes and the team drove to the Center.

With duffle bags and John's lone suitcase, the staff piled into the bus and traveled the short distance to the civilian airplane waiting on the tarmac inside McChord.

It was 5:30 a.m., and the pilot was finishing his pre-flight check. An Airman was standing at the aircraft base, checking off personnel from the manifest. The plane was loaded.

"You can sit anywhere. You are the only ones taking this flight."

Everyone found a seat and buckled in. The chatter stopped when the Alaska Airline flight 873 captain came on the intercom.

"This is your captain speaking; we will be taking off at 0600. You may walk around the cabin until the seatbelt sign comes on, then please return to your seats and buckle in. Thank you."

Baker sat across the aisle from Jason and John. John was the first to speak.

"Colonel, how do you know General Casey?"

"Old Billy and I go back to high school. We both decided to go career in our respective branch of the military. I chose the army because I wanted to be a doctor.

Billy chose the Marine Corps because he wanted to be in Special Ops and loved to tinker with technology. Sometimes, our orders brought us back together, stationed in the same locale.

Billy's career advanced him in rank quicker, I think, because of his MOS, and because he was deep into special operations that were classified.

Like you and Jason, we have been buddies for decades. That is the reason I allowed you to come along. I also have a vested interest."

"Thank you, sir, for your understanding. I think that if we find David, Billy will be with him."

"I agree," replied Baker.

The intercom squawked on.

"Gentlemen, please return to your seats and fasten your seatbelts. We are now ready to taxi to the runway."

A large vehicle hooked up to the jet and pushed gently backward until the plane was lined up on the tarmac to roll forward. The plane rolled down the tarmac making a right-hand turn to line up with the runway.

The captain's radio came on. Then the plane moved across the runway to taxi back to its original spot.

"What's going on?" asked Jason.

"I don't know, but it appears that we are returning to the terminal."

"Gentlemen, unfortunately, the flight has been canceled due to a massive storm heading our way. It will be hitting us within the next half-hour. We are grounded till it is safe to fly."

Chapter 13: *Tension*

"It all fits." said David.

"What the Holy Spirit has been showing me. We are entering into the beginning of the birth pangs. Wars and rumors of wars and this latest attempt to convince Americans that we are under attack is just a precursor to future events that are unfolding right now."

###

Billy motioned to Tracy and Jeffery, and both moved to a secured cabinet located just inside the terrace door. Each carried a headphone equipped with microphones specially modified to pick up human chatter outside the hidden abode. Everyone placed their headsets on and waited for Billy to give further instructions.

"If you can hear anything other than your breathing and heartbeat, they are not fitted correctly. These are invaluable for surveillance and communicating with one another. I will explain later what other goodies are in the headsets." Billy paused, waiting for his pupils to readjust the headgear.

"Okay, is everyone's headset in place?"

Billy signed for everyone to reach behind their left ear and push a button with a gentle push. The sound was deafening as the strength of the frequency was close to a hundred decibels.

Everyone was losing balance and feeling dizzy. Waves of nausea settled in.

"Computer, reduce the volume to seventy-five percent." All were stumbling, trying to regain an upright position, but Billy because he was unaffected by the trauma.

"Computer, reduce the volume to fifty percent."

Nausea left, the spinning stopped, and everyone regained their balance.

"Is everyone okay? Now double-tap the same button."

Conversation from the outside entered their comlinks. The noise sounded like bombs going off, animals fighting, and buses driving away.

No one had expected the nightly APCs, armored personnel carriers, driving around the hills listening for surveillance chatter.

"Billy, what's going on?"

"The usual; Satan's soldiers came out of the schoolhouse you saw earlier today. Of course, the people could not come out unless, you know, with the fake mark!"

"You mean the mark of the beast; the number 666?" asked Jerry. "Right. But I thought that wasn't going to happen until the middle of the seven year tribulation period.

"What about hearing us?" asked David

"Fat chance! Even if I messed something up, God has already promised our safety. I'll turn up the volume to fifty-five percent so you can hear the so-called newcomers to the damned.

They are so eager to follow something that they do not know they will sign an execution order confining them to hell and the lake of fire. The sad part is that they could die today, and their fate would still be the same, even without the mark!

The driver spits out the script they learned to tell their riders the lie. They say that churches used to be so good, but the ones on television want to keep you poor and make them rich!"

"You remember those preachers; you give, I get?" His riders voiced approval. They are so narrow minded! The Bible says that a man cannot love a man and a woman cannot love a woman.

Christians hate how others live, because to them homosexuality is a crime; oh yeah, a sin," said the driver and his riders cheered him as he drove back to the school.

Chapter 14: *Timothy*

Grayson knocked on Sims' door and then entered the office.

"Come in, Tim. What can I do for you, my boy?"

"Well, sir, ah, Isaiah, I am having a problem obtaining the specialists you wanted."

"What seems to be the problem? Are you having second thoughts about our orders?"

"Nothing like that. I've lined up several who are willing to accomplish the task, but…"

"But what!" Sims snapped, cutting off Grayson.

"It's the weather, sir, and logistics. Many of the experts are in Washington State, and there is a sudden and unprecedented storm front moving in. The ones living elsewhere can't get here because the airports are closed in and around Albuquerque."

Sims took off his glasses and sprayed cleaner on the lenses and picked up the blue swath of fabric and cleaned them.

"I guess then if our guys can't make it, their guys can't either. It looks like we have a reprieve, my friend."

"What about the orders, Isaiah?'

"Not to worry, I'm sure the High Council is already aware of the situation. I'll call them. I think now we should move ahead with our plans."

###

Snacks were in the cafeteria, and the tenants swarmed the tables of goodies laced with another dose of drug toxins. There was a unique table for the children. The food had a smaller amount of euphoric agents.

Honey, aren't you hungry? The snacks are now out." asked Jane, Doc's wife.

Everyone was yawning and stretching as they left for their quarters. Jane shuffled the kids to the children's snacks and helped them fill their plates with all kinds of pastries.

Doc did not experience the same euphoria because he had been outside in the fresh air and did not receive the nitrous oxide with the rest of the inhabitants. Though Doc was hungry and thirsty, he declined any refreshments.

"It's all free, you know," snapped a servant. "you don't have to pay for it."

"I know, I'm not hungry right now," he lied. Something bothered him.

"Jane would typically have a fit if the kids grabbed junk food instead of fruit. Now, she was helping them pollute their bodies! 'She is not behaving normally,' he thought. 'Her personality is altered.'

Then it dawned on him. "Everyone is acting the same, which means they are being drugged!' Doc had to reconnect with Pastor Ramone.

"Maybe I'll take something for later, okay?" The servant's smile returned.

He picked up a couple of chocolate donuts and an English Danish and wrapped them in napkins. Coffee, soda pop, juice, and bottled water were available. Doc chose the bottled water but did not trust its purity either.

"Do you want a bag to take it back to your room?"

"Sure, thanks," replied Doc, and he put the items in the brown paper bag. He walked over to the table where his wife and two kids were. They were so entranced in their eating none of them even looked up.

'The pigs have bellied up to the trough,' he thought, 'and they are fattening them up, but for what, and why?'

"What did the Council say?"

"You were right, my boy. The Council said what you did. Perhaps they are premature in assessing the situation.

"Hold off eliminating the high school. That's what the High Council told me."

"They knew the military was stuck?"

"Yes. So. Right call, Tim. We have our stay of execution."

Tim was rubbing his temples, trying to stay off another migraine. Sims pulled a prescription bottle from his desk drawer and handed it to Tim.

"What's this? Oxycontin is your script, Isaiah. I can't take this!"

"I don't like to see you suffer," Sims said in mock sincerity. "Besides, you can't serve me with a migraine, can you?"

Tim gave in and took a pill from the bottle. He placed it on his tongue and washed it down with water.

"Thank you, Isaiah, for your concern. I appreciate it."

"It's quite alright, Tim. Go back to your office and take it easy. Let me know how you are doing in a half hour or so, okay? I don't want to lose my right-hand man to something so simple as a migraine."

Ten minutes later, Sims walked to the outer office and found Tim huddled in the corner, wanting to scream from the paranoia enveloping him. The headache was gone; so was his cognitive ability to reason reality from fantasy. He was hallucinating.

"Tim, what's wrong? Come on, my friend. Let's get you on your couch and cover you up. Everything is going to be fine; you'll see. Now go to sleep." Tim passed out.

Back in his office, Sims picked up the landline.

"Yes, sir, it worked beautifully. The oxycontin got rid of Grayson's migraine." He laughed.

"Operation Devil's Breath is underway. No sir, he won't remember a thing." Sims said and hung up the phone.

Chapter 15: *Flight 873*

Flight 873 rolled slowly down the tarmac reentering its original slot. Everyone was looking to Col. Baker for answers. The cabin depressurized from 8,000 psi back to ground level. A green light flashed over the door signaling the go-ahead to open it.

"I don't have any answers right now, so return to the terminal as per the pilot's request. We'll have to sit this one out until new information develops.

"Oddly, the weather service did not see this front coming!"

"John, I am frustrated too. All we can do now is wait for more reports on the storm."

"Sir, that's little solace considering where my kid brother is during all this chaos. I don't even know if he's still alive!" he said, echoing the same feelings Baker had regarding his best friend.

The captain and flight crew disembarked with their bags, went into the terminal, and headed to the flight crew lounge. Officers and civilians used McChord Air Force Base. Vending machines and snack bars were located inside the building.

The small gate came to life as baristas and restaurants opened for business. John, Jason, and Andre walked to the latte stand and ordered espressos. Finding seats away from the others, the three sat down. Andre has a closer relationship with Jason than he did the others. Jason is his son-in-law.

"You know Jason; you have to work on being more stoic with me in front of other military personnel." He said and chuckled.

"Yes Sir! Is that better, dad?"

"You mean, Katie is your daughter, sir?"

"Amusing, son. Yes, John, Katie is my daughter. Jason never told you? How long have you two been friends?"

"He told me that Katie's dad was a high mucky-muck in the army. Funny, I don't recall you at the wedding."

"It hurt not being there to walk Katie down the aisle. I tried to be there, but the army had other plans. I am a neurosurgeon, John, and there aren't many of us in the service. Sometimes I get called away for emergency surgery on a too unstable soldier.

I can't go into too much detail, but a special forces lieutenant received a wound to the head during a covert extraction. I received orders the night before the kids' wedding and flew to a medical ship in the Mediterranean Sea. The surgery lasted seventeen hours, and I had to remain."

"That had to be tough, sir. Did he make it; I mean the soldier?"

"No, he did not. I knew that the damage was too severe to bring him back to a good quality of life, but I had to try to save him. He was the son of a high mucky-muck, Jason's favorite term. He was also my godson, William Casey the second. That was fifteen years ago, and my heart still aches for that boy.

He was also a marine in Special Ops, just like his father. So, you see, John; I can't lose his father too. Billy, of course, forgave me. He was the one who walked Katie down the aisle while I was trying to save his son."

A tear escaped and trickled down his right cheek. Jason had witnessed countless episodes of his father-in-law's grief over the years and knew to let him work back his composure. Andre took an army issue handkerchief from his pocket and blotted the tears away. He nursed his half-cold latte, not caring about the awkward silence. Sometimes that type of silence is the only remedy to seemingly empty words of comfort though well-meant.

###

The other officers walked around conversing with one another, sitting, standing, and going through the motions trying to escape the restless nature of the 'hurry up and wait' game so common in the military. It was nerve-racking at best. It was 0700 when an airman came into the terminal and handed Colonel Baker a message. Baker motioned for John and Jason, and both followed him over to the rest of the men waiting.

###

"Gentlemen, as you were. I've just received word that due to the nature of the storm and its longevity; we have been ordered to stand down until further notice. Keep in mind that we are still on alert, but all of you should return home and get some rest. The storm front is to last for the next several days." Everyone snapped to attention and saluted the colonel.

"Dismissed."

Chapter 16: *Twenty Years*

David was sipping his coffee waiting for Billy to respond to his question. Jerry smiled and said,

"You haven't shown him yet?"

"I was about to when an incursion protocol was initiated." Everyone laughed.

"You began building this place before you became a Christian, but why?"

"When a person reaches the rank of General things in government policy, especially when the Commander-in-Chief changes so often can become unpredictable. Covert missions and some assignments seemed a bit out there if you know what I mean.

The cold war was never really over. Government spin on news releases was an essential tool to put out misinformation to the public, to get Americans, as well as foreign entities, to believe it was over."

"That is when Billy and I figured that if there was a subversive element in our government, we should have a contingency plan to save as many Americans as possible. That is why we laid plans over twenty years ago to build this complex."

"But you built this place under the premise to save patriots, from what?"

"Communism! Since I became a Christian, I believe that more than ever. Think about it, Tracy. Religious freedom and worshiping God was forbidden, punishable by imprisonment, death, or both. Communism said it was for the good of the many but was a ruse to forbid free-thinking and individuality. It is more prevalent today than during the cold war. And it is now out in the open!"

"What do you think now, Billy, since you became a Christian five years ago?" asked Jeffery.

"There are dark forces within our government manipulating Congress, the Senate, and the House of Representatives. The Democratic Party is now called the Democratic Socialists of America, and socialism is the surrender of free government. Rising against socialism is drilled into us in the military! It is a constant threat to national security."

"So why am I here, Billy? I'm an architect, not a military man or computer whiz kid?"

"I need some structures on the surface to enhance the hunting lodge and throw off suspicion that there is anything else going on. There are other reasons I can't discuss right now, David, so please trust me as a brother in Christ."

Chapter 17: *Lab Rat*

Sims walked into the makeshift hospital room, located in the high school basement, and sat watching his protégé struggle to consciousness. Grayson was unaware of Sims using him as a test subject. The viability of the Devil's Breath depends on Tim's behavior. If all proceeds as expected, the brain-altering drug works. Globally it removes free will from humankind. This chemical agent is more catastrophic than any pandemic contrived by man.

Timothy opened his eyes. "Where am I? The last thing I remember is taking that pill you gave me for my headache."

"You left my office, and I went out to check on you after about ten minutes. I was horrified! There you were in the corner of your office, huddled in a lump on the floor shaking. I called 911. You slipped into unconsciousness before the paramedics got there. I thought you were dying, Tim!"

Sims observed Grayson's demeanor to see if Tim was accepting the lie he was weaving.

Tim felt his head, and it was covered with a bandage where a surgeon carved a wound to simulate a brain operation.

The staples were painful, and Tim's head hurt, but for a different reason other than the migraine. The nurse came in and administered an I.V. injection of morphine. His body surrendered to the drug, leaving him half-conscious.

"The doctor told me that you had a brain aneurism and the pain you were having was the onset of a stroke. You weren't having migraines, Tim; your brain was building up to a massive hemorrhage! If I hadn't called 911 when I did, you would have died!"

"Thank you, Isaiah." He replied, barely able to speak coherently. "I honestly thought I was having migraines again. I had them as a kid, you know. I wonder why I have no paralysis, though. I mean, everyone I ever knew or heard of having a stroke always had some type of it as a residual effect from the stroke."

Sims knew he had to quickly sidestep that truth and fabricate a cleverer lie for Tim to swallow.

"You are fortunate, my boy. The surgeon stopped the bleeding before the brain began to swell."

"That makes sense. Why does my head still hurt?"

"You just had major brain surgery! Do you think that wouldn't hurt?"

"I'm sorry I let you down, Isaiah. You can find another to replace me. I'll understand."

"Nonsense! You'll be out of here in a couple of days. The doctors said that your recovery is nothing short of miraculous! I can manage that long without you. Besides, you and I are a team, right?"

"What about Operation Boom?"

"That's been put on hold indefinitely. The High Council has agreed to move ahead with Operation Devil's Breath. If all goes well, the drug will erase everyone's memories of past events, and no one will have to die for something they can't remember. The plan is moving right on schedule, and the High Council is extremely pleased."

Sims placed his right hand on Tim's arm, trying to show compassion. He looked at him and smiled a reassuring smile, though condescendingly.

"You will be released on Friday morning. You'll have to wear these special dark glasses to protect your eyes for a few days because of the surgery. It's Wednesday afternoon, and I'll personally pick you up and take you back to your apartment at the high school. Get some rest, okay?" Sims left the room and lit up a cigarette.

'That young man is so gullible,' He thought. 'Being raised without a father made it that much easier to pose as a good father figure to him. Beware of wolves dressed in sheep's clothing. He doesn't suspect a thing.'

Sims took a deep drag off his smoke, exhaled, and his demon laughed as he left for the war-room upstairs.

Chapter 18: What Now!

John slammed his suitcase in the seat next to him. His face went from tan to red as his anger built. Jason sat next to Baker, and both left John to his emotional outburst. The bus was again loaded by officers who were now tired and perplexed by the newest developments.

"What now? How can we sit this out!?"

"I don't know, buddy, but the military understands delays. You can bunk at my house until we resume our journey."

"Well, I can't! There has to be another means of transportation!"

"Even if there were, it would take days to get there," said Baker. "I thought about the train service, but by the time we got there, the storm front would have already moved on, and we would arrive too late to help anyone."

"The message said several days, right?"

"John, that's what was predicted by the National Weather Service, but you know as well as I do that weather tracking is not an exact science. The storm could all blow over in a matter of hours."

"Or not! Your buddy is stuck there too, so how can you be so reserved?"

"Hey old buddy, lighten up. Dad did not create the storm!"

"It's okay, Jason; I understand John's grief. I envy you, John. You can voice your opinions and anger openly.

As a colonel, I have to suppress my feelings and project confidence and leadership."

"Sorry, sir, I just thought that we were really on our way to finding David."

"I understand. By the way, you are not in the military. When we are alone, you may call me Andre, but colonel in front of the other officers."

The short trip back to Fort Lewis was silent. The winds had picked up, and the personnel shuffled quickly to collect their gear and head to their cars. Jason and John walked over to the car and stowed their bags. Exhausted, Jason pulled into the driveway, shut off the motor, and the two carried their bags into the house.

Katie had coffee and started another pod in the machine. She set places for the three of them at the kitchen table. Jason dropped his bag at the door, and John took his bag into the spare bedroom. They joined Katie at the table.

"The news on the television reported an hour ago that the weather service issued a weather alert regarding western Washington.

"Julie!" John said. He had been so worried about David he didn't even think about the storm affecting her.

"It's okay, John. I already talked to Julie. She's fine. I also told her that you and Jason would probably be returning to the house until the weather lifted."

"Thanks, Katie. Jason, you go ahead and take the next cup of coffee. I'll make mine after I call Julie." He replied and walked down the hall to the bedroom.

Jason took his coffee and sat beside Katie at the kitchen table. They drank their coffees in silence.

It was 9:30 a.m. as John dialed Julie's cell phone. One ring, two rings, and a third one resonated in his ear. No answer and her voice mail did not pick up the call. Now John had two people to worry over.

Chapter19: *Sanctuary*

Everything is running correctly." said Jerry as he keyed in the last few strokes on the keyboard.

"The lower floors are now in service. The electricity, water, heating, cooling systems for each floor, and the animal shelters, are now operating at full capacity. The hydroponics are up and running proficiently, and sun tubes are now open."

Billy had been dreaming of this day for ten long years. Countless contractors, all signing an affidavit of non-disclosure to anyone, were contracted. It is deemed 'Top Secret.' He watched as each floor lit from the darkness. Cobwebs hung on the surveillance lens in the halls and rooms.

Billy keyed in instructions to clear the atmosphere with a mist of fresh scents of the desert flowers erasing the old musty smell, denoting being closed for so long. All the lower levels were on minimal automated maintenance to keep the atmosphere from mass condensation.

Lights flashed on, and the cleaning crew-Billy's guests from the lodge-scoured their new home with the precision of an artist. Young men and women dusted, mopped, and swept away any traces of age and transformed the lower sanctuary into a beautiful, spotless domicile where anyone would want to live.

The crew were all Christians and loved the Lord. They believed as old Billy. A civil war was coming in America, and the fight for freedom against tyranny and the communist threat was more pervasive than ever.

The freedom to worship Jesus Christ and the Almighty God had reached critical mass with no possibility of conquering such a threat. America seemed to be a dying country. God Forbid!

"Billy, where did you meet all the people who are sprucing up all the lower levels?" asked Jerry as he watched the security monitors.

"I did a lot of praying before I ever considered bringing more personnel on board. Carlos suggested some of our church members. So prayerfully, a call went out to the congregation, and the response was overwhelming. God showed me that we needed our fellow believers to help before the rapture so our temporary home could be blessed, prayed over, and protected.

That way, the door will open for those who accept Jesus after the rapture to have a safe place to live as they spread the gospel of Jesus Christ. The enemy calls their practice dry runs; ours is called praise and worship!"

###

"Billy, brunch is ready." said Tracy.

The two left the computer room and entered the elevator. Billy slid a plastic key into the slot and the doors closed. He keyed in a code that raised the lift to the basement level.

As they entered the common room, the smells of baked quiche, fresh bacon, and coffee wafted through the corridors and out onto the balcony.

"David, are you enjoying learning about this sanctuary?"

"There's so much, Billy. It is like every architect's dream to design and build a super modern and secure facility like this one! I have just finished the virtual tour of the first floor and can't wait to see the rest of it."

"Billy and Jerry smiled.

"You haven't seen anything yet! It is God who orchestrated all of it!" said Jerry.

The three went into the common room where the dining table had been expanded and set for brunch. The white tablecloth was gone and replaced with a small floral print and disposable dishes; a setting far removed from the night's formal setting before.

"Jeffery and I are going to town after lunch to lay in more supplies. That's why the disposable dishes. Sorry."

"It's strange that business is as usual in Albuquerque. I am sure that the city has experienced confusion and panic to some degree. At any rate, we should be gone for two to three hours at most." said Jeffery.

Everything was precut and set on the table. Billy's exceptional coffee and Jeffery's creamers were always the finishing touches to an already delightful dining experience, whether paper plates or China, the meals were still incredible.

After brunch, everyone threw the paper dishes in the trash can outside the kitchen door. Tracy set up coffee and creamer, along with cookies, out on the terrace.

The kitchen once again sparkled, and the husband-wife duo left but not before Billy prayed over them for a safe journey there and back. One could never be too careful these days.

Jeffery grabbed the keys to their SUV and sped off toward town. It was unknown what they would find there. Jeffery took Tracy's hand and kissed it as he drove.

"Don't worry, honey, God is with us. We will be okay."

She smiled and squeezed his hand.

David, Billy, and Jerry moved out onto the balcony. The conversation centered around the bombs and what was going on in the school.

The room turned to darkness. David's friends' voices became softer until he could hear nothing.

"David!" yelled Billy.

David crumpled to the floor.

"Jerry, call the EMT team from the sanctuary!"

Chapter 20: *Doc*

"Where are you going, Doc?"

"I need some fresh air. I thought I'd go outside for a bit and talk to some of the guards. Maybe one of them can let me know how much longer we will have to stay here."

"Does it matter? We have food, shelter, clean clothes, and a warm bed to sleep in; what more do we need?" she turned and went to the bedroom.

'Our freedom.' Doc thought and walked outside.

Jane didn't know that Doc had the food in a bag he tucked inside his shirt. 'If I could just find pastor Ramone. I could pass the food off to him and have it analyzed for drug toxins.'

Doc saw a small group of believers outside the fence, praying for the people inside. A guard approached him and engaged in friendly conversation with him.

"Are you okay?"

"I'm fine, just needed a little air. Have you seen any animal attacks?"

"Nah, I think that it's a bunch of horse manure. None of the guys outside the fence has seen anything either. They said they heard dogs fighting, but that could be a recording to scare people." The corporal laughed.

"Oh well, orders are orders. Right? And we have been assigned to protect all of you from those savage beasts. But what about the bombs? I think they are scarier than animals."

"I've been thinking the same thing. The bombs exploding are far more serious than a few dogs looking for food. Hey, any idea when we can return to our homes?"

"Who knows, we don't. Have a good one." said the soldier and walked on.

Doc continued his hike around the fence. He turned the corner and saw a large group in prayer. As he crept closer, he recognized the leader, Pastor Ramone. Doc stood waiting for the group to disperse and approached the fence.

"Pastor, got a minute?"

"Always. What's going on, Doc?"

"I've been thinking about what you said yesterday. After the soldier rushed me back inside, I saw something that didn't seem right."

"How so?"

"Well, I saw my wife and two kids leaving our room, and they seemed lethargic and had difficulty waking up. I looked around the cafeteria, and everyone there had the same expression. Then the snacks were out, and it was like watching a herd of swine racing to the troughs to eat."

"What are you thinking?"

"I'm not sure. But I was a medic in the military, and I noticed that everyone inside the school act like they hadn't eaten in days. Jane, my wife, would go ballistic if the kids tried to eat junk instead of healthy foods.

The servers set up a different table for the kids with the same kind of snacks on it, and she was leading the way to junk food. For her, this is not normal behavior."

"That is unusual for a person to act so hungry."

"There's more. Jane confronted me when I wasn't eating, which drew one of the server's attention. He admonished me, saying the food was free and I was rude for not eating. So, I took some food to take back to my room to eat later. Then the server's smile returned. He even offered me a bag." said Doc.

He discreetly handed it to Ramone through the fence.

"Hide it quickly…"

He took the donuts from Doc and slid them inside his shirt.

"Do you think they are using drugs on the people inside the high school? I know that the food manufacturers put flavor enhancers to quote-unquote make the flavors taste better. The so-called health foods make a person crave more." Asked Ramone.

"Dude, I don't know! But I'm telling you this much if the body doesn't get the signal that it's full, that person continues to eat themselves into misery. The more they eat, the more they want."

"I think I understand, Doc. I'll have my wife test it for drug toxins."

"If the enzyme to stop the 'I'm not hungry' feeling is present, then what else are they feeding us to get it into our systems? There has got to be a drug they are preparing for us to ingest. But for what reason? And could it be deadly?"

"Understood. I wish you'd reconsider hearing the story of Jesus again."

The hostile soldier came around the corner.

"Please take this track and read it for yourself." Pastor Ramone handed it through the fence, and the soldier snatched it from Ramone's hand. "Hey, thanks. You people are all alike! You are so pushy trying to get others to fall for your fairytales." Doc smiled at Ramone. He walked away, leaving the soldier standing with the Jesus story tract in his hand.

Chapter 21: *Pick Up!*

Come on Julie, pick up!" John said into his cell phone. "Turn off your headset and…"

"Hello, John?"

"Where have you been?! I called you at 9:30, 10:30 and now it's 12:30 p.m. Are you alright? The storm had me worried."

"Calm down, honey; I was in the studio. And yes, I'm fine. Thank you for asking." She was a little annoyed with John's attitude.

"I'm sorry, Julie. But the storm has me concerned about your safety."

"This is Washington State. We have weather like this regularly, so why are you so worried?"

"Not like this one; it came up out of nowhere! "We've been grounded until further notice."

"I know Katie told me. I also called your colleagues, and they agreed to take on your patients until you get back. And John, they both said to take as long as you need to find your brother."

"You've always got my back, babe. I love you. I'm glad you're fine. But do me a favor. Leave your headphones off till the storm passes so that I can get ahold of you? Okay?"

"Yes, dear, will do. The news said that the weather should be breaking within the next couple of days."

"That's good to hear. I'll keep you posted…"

John walked back into the kitchen where Katie and Jason were getting ready for lunch. Chicken salad sandwiches and coffee were sitting on the table. They sat down and doctored their coffees and ate in relative silence. After lunch, Jason and John went into the living room after refilling coffees. Katie joined the two men.

"How's Julie doing?"

"She's fine. She also reminded me that Washington State always has unpredictable weather. She also promised to keep her headphones off so I can reach her."

"I told you she was okay, John. I don't know why you didn't believe me," said Katie, winking.

"I know. I know. But I had to hear Julie's voice again. She always has a way of calming me down. Jason, have you heard anything from your dad yet?"

"Unfortunately, no, but I'm sure he is just as anxious as you are."

Katie's cell phone rang.

"Hi, dad. I'm fine. Jason and John are here, and we just finished lunch. Really? Jason, dad wants you to turn your blankety-blank cell phone on so he can call you!"

Jason's phone blared on, and the ringer seemed to share the colonel's frustration.

"Okay, Private!" Baker yelled into the phone.

"Sorry, sir, I turned it off when we were on the plane. Wait, did you say Private?"

"Yes, I did! You and John get your butts over to McChord!

ASAP! The rest of the team are already on their way."

"On our way, dad. Sorry, how long have you been trying to call me?"

"This was the first time. I had already called my aide to contact the others." Baker chuckled under his breath.

"Thanks a lot, dad." replied Jason and hung up.

"Grab your gear, John; it's a go for the Air Force Base."

The two rushed out the door as Jason gave Katie a hit-and-run kiss. They sped down the residential area, spewed out into the after-lunch traffic, and headed to McChord.

Jason flashed his credentials at the gate checkpoint and drove to the terminal where the commercial jet was waiting.

He saw his father-in-law climbing out of his car, and Jason parked beside him. They were the first ones to arrive.

Colonel Baker looked at the two and smiled. He greeted them as they pulled their gear out of the car and slipped inside the terminal.

The flight crew had already arrived and were on their way to the plane's cockpit.

"I'm guessing that you called us first, right colonel.?"

"That's affirmative. How bad do you think it would look if the colonel's son-in-law were the last one to get here?"

"Right, I know, dad. Anyway, I take it the storm has cleared enough for us to get underway."

"Within the next hour or two, hopefully. At least when it does, the team will be ready."

"John, did you reach your wife and find out how hard the storm hit Seattle?"

"That's the strange part colonel, Julie said that the wind was blowing, but not like here. She also said that it didn't last long either."

“That’s odd. Anything on the news detailing the storm’s epicenter?”

“The National Weather Service stated that the storm centered more south from Tacoma down to Olympia. Its heaviest concentration was around Fort Lewis and McChord Air Force base.

“Yes, it’s very odd, Jason,” said Baker.

John’s hair bristled on the back of his neck. He sensed that God had intervened, though he hadn’t spoken to Him in years. David always followed God. It drove John nuts. He couldn’t stop thinking about what David said.

‘There are no accidents where God is concerned, and everything happens by His design.”

Jason and the colonel were busy with the customary salutes and handshakes, leaving John immersed in his thoughts. He remembered how he teased David for being such a staunch believer.

“John, I don’t get it. We grew up in the same house with the same parents. How can you be so flippant regarding your beliefs in God?”

John recalled the conversation repeatedly, and it was very annoying. His replies became more sarcastic.

‘Maybe I was adopted!’ he thought, telling David the flip side of being adopted. David never got upset with him. He always seemed to remain calm and continued his preaching to John.

‘Maybe David was sincere after all.’ He thought.

‘Could there be something valid to all this Jesus stuff that David believes so strongly? That storm was too weird to be a coincidence. And now it’s safe to travel? Or is it? What next?’

He climbed aboard flight 873 for another attempt to get airborne.

‘I guess we’ll see.’ he thought and settled back in his first-class seat.

Chapter 22: *Gennicy*

"Hi daddy," said his young brunette daughter and kissed Billy on the cheek.

"How's David doing?"

"I'm not sure, While we were out the balcony talking to David, his eyes rolled back in his head, and he collapsed onto the floor.

One of the cleaning crew's wife is a Nurse Practitioner and thinks that David has post concussive syndrome. He has been complaining from a headache.

"Did you tell him I was coming?" she asked staring at him through deep brown eyes.

"No, Gennicy, I did not tell him that you were even my daughter or that you became a doctor." replied Billy in mock anger."

"Was he hurt during the recent explosions?"

"He had a head injury and some scrapes and bruises. And he complained about headaches."

"That's it! He had a concussion, and that is why the headaches. Did the hospital check him out?"

"David said that a couple of medics found him coming to, in the dirt, and they dressed his wounds. They also encouraged him to go inside the school to see a doctor there. He declined."

Gennicy opened the door and entered the room where the man she loved lay unconscious with I.V. tubes everywhere.

She brushed away the tears and went to work on David taking his vitals and drawing blood samples. All she could do now is wait for the test results and pray he wouldn't go into a vegetative state.

Gennicy sat at the table in David's room nursing a cup of tan coffee that Billy had made for her.

She thought back on the last time she and David were together. They never broke up; they just parted company so Gennicy could return home and take care of her mom. She remembered their parting words.

"I don't want to leave you, David, but I have to so I can take care of my mom."

She cried and clung to David's embrace. His kindness made it more difficult to depart.

"It's going to be alright, Genn," he replied as he stroked her shoulder-length hair. Your mom and dad need you. Besides, we are only a phone call away. Right?"

She never called him because she focused on her mother dying from cancer.

"He'll never talk to me again," she said out loud, not meaning to verbalize.

Billy was sitting by her, reading his Bible. He looked up and set it on the table next to him. He hugged and kissed Gennicy.

"That couldn't be further from the truth. You do know David never dated or was interested in anyone else. Right?"

"Yes, daddy, I know. We agreed that if it were God's will for us to be together, that it would happen."

"Well, there you go. Stop fretting over something that God is controlling, okay?" He kissed her on the cheek.

"Your mother would be so proud of you."

Chapter 23: *Confirmed*

Doc dressed. He allowed Jane and the kids to go into the cafeteria without him. They hadn't noticed that he purposely hung back so he could slip outside without being noticed. It was 8:00 A.M., Friday morning, and the guards had not yet arrived inside the fence.

He navigated around the perimeter and saw Ramone standing near the fence toward the property's back. Ramone motioned Doc to follow him to the back gate, which was partially open and handed him a bag of bottled water and sandwiches from the church.

"You were right," Ramone said. "The food has drugs in it. Those donuts you gave me are full of toxins. My wife, Susan, said that Scopolamine, is for nausea in small doses. In more significant amounts, she did say it had addictive properties like heroin.

"I suggest that you find a private place, eat a couple of sandwiches, and drink the bottled water I gave you. It could also be in the bottled water they are dispensing to everyone inside."

"What about my family, pastor? How do I detoxify them and get us out of there?"

"I'm working on it. My entire church is praying for you and everyone else inside the school."

"Far out! But I can't come out every day getting food from you and not eating what is quote-unquote, 'free.' Someone is bound to get suspicious, and who knows what will happen. That pushy guard is also watching us."

"If you can meet me here early in the morning before the troops arrive, I can smuggle food to you and enough for your family.

Also, put this menthol rub up against your nostrils and use this mask to keep from breathing in the gases filtering into your room."

Doc took the bag and slid it under his jacket. "Why are you helping me, Rev.?"

"It's simple. God does not want anyone to perish. All of us deserve death for our sins, but His Son, Jesus Christ, took our punishment for us."

"So, you're saying that all I have to do is admit I'm a sinner and believed that Jesus died for me? Is that it?"

"Not quite. The moment Christ died, the temple veil ripped from top to bottom, and a major earthquake shook the land. After Jesus died on the cross, God raised Him from the dead and on the third day, God sat him at His right hand."

"The doorway to redemption is now open but is only available through the belief that Jesus is the Son of God and that God raised him from the dead. Jesus not only destroyed sin for us, but he also conquered death, the final consequence for sin."

"What are you doing out here!?" a familiar voice snapped.

Doc turned and saw the soldier that had been harassing him.

"Are you on some kind of power trip? None of the other guards said that Martial Law was in effect!"

The guard was dumbfounded, and red-faced that anyone would call his bluff.

He raised his AR-15 and drew a bead on Doc. Then he lowered his weapon and left, rushing past another guard.

Chapter 24: *Take Off*

Everyone was buckled in their seats and the captain received final clearance for take-off. The jet raced down the runway, gaining speed to become airborne. Near the end of the runway, the plane lifted off the ground. Angling upwards towards the heavens, it leveled at thirty-thousand feet.

The seatbelt sign went off, and some cabin occupants stood up to stretch. The beverage cart moved down the aisle. The flight attendant offered coffee, juice, and water, but no alcohol on this flight.

John felt pensive as he sat in his seat. Something was not right. Was David alive but injured somehow? The cart stopped by him, and John took a cup of coffee.

He remembered when mom and dad had gotten into the car accident; he felt the same uneasiness with David as he did with his parents.

It did not console him. Their parents did not make it, and the funeral was tough on both. David tried to comfort John, explaining that mom and dad were in heaven with Jesus.

"It was their time to go home." He said. "John, mom, and dad are happy. They aren't suffering from their earthly bodies because their bodies are now perfect."

'I wish I could believe that David.' He thought. 'I miss them terribly.' John sunk back in his seat.

He hadn't sat by Jason and Andrea and had chosen a seat isolated from the others so he could be alone in his thoughts. They walked over to John and sat down by him. John straightened his posture. He knew Jason and Andrea were concerned.

"John, what's going on, buddy? We're on our way. You should be relieved." said Jason and put his hand on John's shoulder.

"I am, but we started out on Wednesday, and it's now Friday, and I'm no closer to locating my brother than I was on Wednesday." John sunk back in his seat again.

"I'm feeling the same way. I feel like something is going on that could be bad, but I don't know what," said Andre.

John looked out the window to gather his thoughts.

"You're probably going to think I'm crazy but, I've felt that David is in trouble and is injured or something. We both felt that same way the night our parents were killed by a drunk driver."

"Sorry, bro, I remember that night. You and David were visiting Katie and me when you got the call. Everything seemed like they were going to pull through, and suddenly both died from their injuries and within hours apart."

"I used to think that as a neuro-surgeon, such events or feelings were the imaginings of grief-stricken individuals not knowing how to handle tragedy. But over the years, and hearing stories about people dying and coming back from the dead, I have had to rethink the possibility that these events occurred, especially in combat situations."

The three sat silent for several minutes. The plane began to toss and jumble as it flew through dense clouds and turbulence.

A drop of five hundred feet in altitude gave the occupants a brief feeling of weightlessness. The seatbelt sign flashed on, and the intercom squawked.

"Gentlemen, we are experiencing some unusually rough weather at altitude. Please make sure your seatbelts are secured, and do not leave your seats. This flight could be a very bumpy ride."

The flight attendant pushed the beverage cart into its locked compartment and fastened his seatbelt. The plane plunged again, and the oxygen masks dropped down.

"For your safety," began the captain, "please put on the masks and leave them in place. The cabin pressure is fluctuating, and I'm attempting to correct the problem."

Everyone complied and placed their masks on their faces. Another dip in altitude and compartments flew open, ejecting personal belongings stowed above.

Chapter 25: *Unconscious*

Jerry came into the room and walked over to Gennicy.

"How's he doing?"

"Hi, Uncle Jerry. He's still unconscious but is stable."

"That's good news, right?" he asked.

"Yes and no. David is in a coma, but the longer he is in the coma, the less likely he will come out of it if he comes out of it at all."

Jerry hugged her and said,

"Spoken like a true physician. Hey kiddo, you know that our God is the supreme physician, and miracles happen all the time."

"Thanks, Uncle Jerry. I needed that."

"With that said, I've got some news from the outside world. It appears that the explosions are happening in the southwest and nowhere else.

The rest of the country is business as usual."

"So, we are not at war or even close?"

"Not at all. The news media reports that old World War II bombs left in storage explode at random. They also say that there is a blackout on cell towers and satellite arrays to prevent more bombs from exploding. And the rest of the world is buying that junk?"

"Of course they are, Jerry. It's government spin at its best." Billy replied.

"During the cold war, the United States government tailored reports with the press to fit national security needs and manipulate the American population. It led the people to agree with whatever the government had planned, be it war or peace. It was an effective tool in the past and is now indispensable in these latter days."

"If I remember my history, isn't that called propaganda?" asked Gennicy.

"Of course it is, honey; governments couldn't get the people to do what they wanted without it. A world without God means a world of evil, lies, and deceit."

"The intercom came to life.

"Where is everyone? We got back and unloaded the supplies, and no one was around."

"Anyway, we've got some disturbing news for you. Coffee and snacks are on the terrace."

"We're in David's room down in the infirmary, Tracy. He collapsed and is in a coma."

"He is stable for now, and Gennicy is taking care of him," said Billy.

"We're on our way back upstairs."

Jerry transferred a camera app to Gennicy's smartwatch and persuaded her to go upstairs and eat something. Tracy met them with a tray of tuna sandwiches and fruit cups. Water, coffee, and milk were already resting on the table.

As they sat and ate, Tracy and Jeffery filled them in on Albuquerque's situation.

"I thought the National Guard would be everywhere, thinking there would be no traffic lights, mass hysteria, looting, and more." Jeffery began.

"It was not like that at all!" said Tracy.

"We thought that the guard would stop us, but there weren't any around. The city was carrying on as if nothing had happened. There were no runs on the supermarkets, no lines from shortages because there wasn't any!"

"That makes sense," said Jerry. "I was able to get a signal and saw the same thing nationwide. It is business as usual everywhere else accept our little community."

"Then David's visions are all true, and the area where we are is a test run for the evil that is about to be unveiled," said Billy.

Gennicy's watch beeped, and she saw David move his left hand to his head. "He's waking up!" she said and ran to the elevator. She stepped inside, and the door closed behind her. She was shaking, not knowing what to expect. The elevator took forever to descend to level two.

Chapter 26: *Suspect*

Tim got up early and went to the bathroom to get his morning pain meds. The pain seemed a little less, and he pondered whether to take it.

The prescription read: Morphine Sulfate HCL. 10 mgs. Take one tablet four times a day as needed for pain.

'That's every six hours.' He thought. 'My head doesn't hurt that bad that I need Morphine. I think I'll hold off.'

He put the bottle back in the medicine cabinet and walked into the living room. A caregiver was already there preparing breakfast. He brought a steaming cup of coffee to Tim. The man knew what he liked in his coffee; lots of cream and sugar.

Bacon, scrambled eggs, hash browns, and sourdough toast were the morning menu. Tim sat at the dining table, sipping his coffee.

"Did you have a good nap?"

"I did, thanks. Who are you?"

"Oh, I'm sorry. My name is Frank. Mr. Sims thought you might need help for a few days, and he hired me to take care of you. I'm a caregiver, so if you have any problems with your pain, need a nap, or anything, I'm here to help and, I also make sure that you take your meds. What time did you take your morning dose?"

"Uh, at 8 a.m." Tim lied. He didn't like the idea of someone else controlling his taking meds. It would be difficult to skip a dose without Frank's knowledge.

Tim sat eating his breakfast, and the front door opened. Sims walked in with flowers and chocolates. He smiled.

"I thought these would lift your spirits," he said and handed them to Frank.

"You are looking much better today."

"Thank you, Isaiah. And thank you for Frank, but I don't think…"

"You need a caregiver? Yes, you do. You are recovering from brain surgery! You are going to be a little shaky for a few days."

"I guess you are right, as usual, Isaiah."

Tim began faking grogginess from the morphine tablet.

"Forgive me; my meds are making me sleepy. I'll be right back; I have to use the bathroom."

Timothy walked into the bathroom and locked the door behind him. He took the pill bottle out of the cabinet, withdrew a pill, and tossed it into the toilet.

His suspicions were correct. He overheard Sims telling Frank to be sure and count his pills.

"We don't want him to stop taking them too soon.

"Tim, I have to go, but I'll see you later, my boy."

"Okay," he said and went into the bedroom to lie down. Something was going on, and it had everything to do with those pills.

Chapter 27: *Shaken*

The plane shook violently as if to break apart. As suddenly as the crisis began, it stopped; the cabin pressure returned to normal, and the shaking ceased. The jet was once again flying smoothly.

Everyone looked at each other, wondering what had happened. But for a few brief moments, it felt like something, or someone was pushing the plane downward.

"Gentlemen, the cabin pressure has stabilized, and you can remove your masks. It looks like the worst is over, and I do not see any further disturbances on the radar.

We will be landing in Albuquerque, New Mexico, in approximately six-hour and forty-five minutes, including the layover for refueling."

The flight attendant unbuckled and loaded the cart with fresh coffee and beverages, and deli sandwiches supplied by the officer's mess.

Roast beef, Reubens, Black Forest Ham and Cheese, and Turkey sandwiches were available along with potato chips and other snack choices. The support officers ordered their favorites.

John didn't feel like eating, but Jason and Andre's looks persuaded him otherwise.

"I'll have a roast beef, coke, and potato chips," he said. The attendant handed him his order and moved to Jason and Andre sitting across from John.

Two hours had elapsed since the harrowing experience, and the trash was picked up. The team was quietly talking, reading, or napping for the rest of the ride.

"This is your captain speaking…"

"Now what!?" barked John.

"I have just been informed that Albuquerque International Airport has been closed. Our new destination is Santa Fe Municipal Airport, which is the closest airport that's operational near Albuquerque, New Mexico. Sorry folks."

John kicked the empty seat in front of him and cursed under his breath, then asked, "How far away is Santa Fe from Albuquerque?"

"Fifty-six miles southeast from there." replied Baker in his colonel's voice.

"That's just great!" yelled John and punched the seat.

Chapter 28: *In the Spirit*

"Am I dead?" Asked David.

"No, you are not, but your body is in a deep sleep. In the physical realm, it is called a coma. The Almighty wants you to return to your body. Spread the news of what is taking place inside the school. The urgency is great!"

"What can I do? I'm not inside the school except when you take me there."

"David, your obedience by not going in saved your life. Did you see any fellow believers entering the gates?"

"No, not really," he replied.

"What do you think would happen to a believer if discovered?" asked the Spirit.

"You don't mean they would kill them, do you?"

"We are talking about the destruction of humanity. Do you honestly think that one lone Christian taken out of the way would bother them? Not! The more believers that die will make it easier for evil to rule."

"You have been with me on several occasions and have witnessed everything done to Timothy Grayson. You saw him go from a migraine to a skull fracture and incision to fake a brain operation. And it is all an experiment!" he said. "Will I remember all that I have witnessed?"

"Every detail. Come, it is time to return you."

David was no longer in the War Room at the high school but was standing at his bed, staring at his unconscious body. He saw Gennicy rush in; David was back in his body, stroking Gennicy's hair as she laid her head on David's shoulder.

"Shush. It's going to be okay, my love. I'll always be here for you," said David She burst into tears and kissed David's forehead.

"Oh God, thank you for bringing him back!" David and Gennicy were hugging each other. "Daddy, look! he's okay!"

"How are you feeling, David?"

"I'm weak and feel like I haven't slept in days. It's so good to see you, Genn."

Dr. Casey composed herself and ran the routine exams and tests for someone who'd been in a coma. He hadn't eaten, but the I.V. fluids kept David hydrated.

"Will someone get these tubes out of me so I can get dressed and get something to eat?"

"Not so fast, Mr. driver personality," said Genn with a big smile.

"Your body went through a major trauma, and you need to rest a while before you get out of here."

"Ah Doc! Can't I at least have something to eat? He replied in a playful whine.

"Okay, I'll have Jeffery make you some soup and a half-a - sandwich."

"Coffee?" he pleaded. "Come on Genn, it's your dad's private stock."

"Maybe, but only two cups, for now," she smiled and walked out.

Billy and Jerry remained behind and told David what had been happening.

"Tracy and Jeffery came back and told us that it was business as usual in Albuquerque. There was no National Guard, no looting, no food shortages, and everything seemed eerily normal.

They returned right after you had collapsed and were brought to the infirmary."

"I got a signal from the clamshell connection and found out that the only place where there were any disturbances is in and around where we are.

The rest of the world is being told-via the news media- that WWII bombs are exploding with no warning." said Jerry.

"You had us worried, my friend."

"Thank you for your concerns, but I wasn't in a coma.

The Holy Spirit took me away again and showed me what the future faces, and it is grim. We must act immediately! He showed me what the dark forces are planning within the next several days. There is an extreme danger for the people inside the high school."

"What did you see?" asked Billy.

"Do you know anything about a drug called; "Devil's Breath?"

Billy turned ashen and had to sit down.

"It's happening again," he said, placing his head in his hands.

Chapter 29: *A Plan*

Doc entered his room and saw that his family had not yet returned from breakfast. He pulled out a sandwich and quickly ate it, swirling down each bite with water Ramone gave him. They were peanut butter and jelly, something that wouldn't spoil fast. He thought about everything the pastor told him as he ate a second sandwich.

'I'm so hungry,' he thought.

'This food and water taste different than the stuff served in the school.' He stowed the rest of the sandwiches in his coat and not his pillow so the cleaning staff would not find his stash.

The door slid open, and his sluggish wife and children walked in.

"I'm exhausted," said Jane, feeling the effects of the increased doses of the mysterious drug in her food.

"I think I need a nap."

The kids had already gone to their bedrooms and laid down. Jane waved to her husband as she entered hers and the doors slid shut.

'This is my chance.'

He went to the bathroom and put some menthol inside each nostril that Ramone gave him. Doc went back into the living room with his mask in place. Five minutes later, he noticed there was no smell of gas pumping into the rooms.

The door popped open, and the maid walked in. Since she was new, she hadn't been instructed not to enter rooms during the sleep period. Doc jumped, startled at her entry.

"Oh, I'm sorry." she said. "I didn't know anyone was here."

"What time are you supposed to clean our rooms?" asked Doc, reflecting irritation in his voice.

"10:00 a.m.," she replied.

"Well, it's only 9: a.m.! Check your watch. What time does it say?"

"It's 10:00 a. m.," she replied sheepishly.

"I forgot to set it back one hour to your time zone."

"I won't report you this time, but I suggest that you reset your watch so that it won't happen again."

She nodded and left his apartment.

Doc then checked to see if there were any hidden cameras inside his temporary abode. There were none.

"Man, I thought sure the guards had found out about my stash and were coming to bust me."

He sat back on the sofa and drank more bottled water.

'That was too close.' He thought.

'Since that happened, I have a time when they check for contra band items. No cameras are in the rooms. Sweet, I think I can go out and start smuggling food into my family.

'I have got to get us out of here. But why is there no gas coming in?'

Chapter 30: *Diverted*

"Gentlemen, we are two hours out from landing at Santa Fe Regional Airport. I have instructed the flight captain to notify Kirtland Air Force Base to dispatch jeeps, medical supplies, and emergency survival equipment. They should arrive in Santa Fe at approximately the same time we touch down. Are there any questions?"

"Sir, do we have any intel as to what we will encounter once we engage our emergency protocols?" asked a Captain.

"No intel," replied Baker. "We have to assume that we are about to enter a hot zone; There is every reason to believe that the area is still unstable from the bombs."

"Sir," asked another officer, "should we expect casualties?"

Baker hesitated because of John's brother and Billy.

"At this juncture, gentleman, we should be prepared for any contingency. For now, I suggest that you get as much sleep as possible. There is no guarantee you'll get any after we land."

John pushed the call button for the flight attendant. The attendant made his way toward the front of the cabin.

"May I help you?"

"Yes, thanks; I'd like a cup of coffee and lots of creamer."

"Hey, you heard the colonel. Get some sleep!" chided Jason grinning.

"I wish I could, but the closer we get to Albuquerque, the more nervous I am about finding David."

Baker also added an order of coffee.

"Not you too, Colonel," said Jason.

"I know how John feels. I'm worried about Billy, too."

"Well, I guess I need some shut-eye for the three of us. Someone in this family has to be alert." Jason replied and winked. He pushed his first-class seat back and closed his eyes.

A brief time later, Jason, John, Baker, and the rest of the team were asleep.

The captain came out of the cockpit and nudged Colonel Baker to follow him back inside.

"Colonel, I wanted to talk to you privately and not over the intercom."

"What's going on, captain? Are we being diverted again?"

"No, nothing like that. Sir, the chatter I've been picking up is extremely unusual."

"How do you mean?"

The aircraft chatter from other pilots has stated that planes have been going and coming all day long at Albuquerque airport."

"Captain, either the airport is closed or open, which is it?"

"That's just it, sir, I've contacted the Albuquerque tower, and the tower states that the airport is closed and to proceed to my alternate destination."

"That is strange. If your instructions are to go to Santa Fe, you should continue there. We have no idea if the chatter is credible."

"Right, that's what I thought, and it's why I wanted your input. We are an hour and fifty-eight minutes out from Santa Fe, and the ground team will reach you on or a little after we land, sir. And colonel, thanks for your help."

"Thanks for your discretion," Baker said and walked back to his seat.

"Dad, is everything okay?"

Chapter 31: *It's Happening Again*

Billy what's wrong?" asked David.

"What do you mean 'It's happening again?'"

Billy looked up and saw the expressions on Jerry and David's faces.

"Years ago, too many of them, I was assigned to a special ops group researching the human mind. The purpose was to find an agent that could be introduced into the body and render the person's will useless."

"How could that be possible? What about the Geneva Convention?"

"Do you think for one moment that Adolf Hitler cared about human rights?

His circle of friends included Satanists, witches, and sorcerers, in other words, the occult. He wanted to create a super-race of people, and anyone who was not white was in serious jeopardy."

Gennicy walked in and brought David a cup of chicken noodle soup and half of a tuna sandwich. She also brought David a cup of her dad's exceptional coffee. She set the tray on David's bedside table.

"You've got to be kidding! This serving is a child's portion!"

"And you are lucky you are getting this much! We'll see about more later.

"So, what did I miss while I was gone? she asked.

"Daddy, you looked depressed."

"Worried is a better word."

"In the thirties before the second world war, a drug arrived in the late 1800's early 1900's. It was believed as a panacea of all drugs, rendering the recipient into a twilight sleep.

During labor, doctors gave women a cocktail of this drug mixed with morphine and chloroform. They would deliver their baby and not remember the pain and what happened during labor."

"So, what's the connection with the "Devil's Breath? It certainly sounds like a miracle drug."

"One would think so, Jerry. Doctors soon realized that when they asked questions during labor, the women not only volunteered the truth but wanted to tell more. It was involuntary."

"Daddy, you weren't born until 1952. How do you know all this? Never mind, the military, right?"

"Correct," he said and smiled at her.

"In the twenties, the Counter-Intelligence Agency, aka, the CIA, caught wind of it and began experiments with the drug.

The CIA discovered that giving the drug to spies caused them to surrender their entire will to their interrogators, and did they not remember a thing."

"In answer to your question Jerry, the Devil's Breath is the street name for Scopolamine."

Billy looked at David, who became nauseous from the headache and the food.

"Are you hurting?"

"Since I came to, I've been hurting; it's a headache mostly, but the rest of my body aches, and I am feeling sick to my stomach."

"That's normal. I'll give you something for it."

She left the room and returned with a hypodermic filled with a pain cocktail to ease his suffering and nausea and injected it into the I.V.

"Sweet dreams," she said, as David succumbed to the drugs.

"He'll sleep for a few hours. Maybe we should move our conversation to the common room. Okay, daddy?"

David slipped into a peaceful slumber. He was now asleep and not in a coma.

Gennicy, Billy, and Jerry left the room so he could rest. It was now late afternoon, and Jeffery and Tracy finished prepping lunch. Coffee was already sitting on the dining table, awaiting food accompaniments.

"Your timing is perfect; lunch is ready. How is David?" asked Tracy.

"I gave him a sedative so he could rest. He is still experiencing a painful return from the concussion."

While the others ate lunch, David was again spirited away by the Holy Spirit. This time was different from the others. This time, he went to heaven.

Chapter 32: *High Council*

That's right, Damon," said Sims. "We launched Operation Devil's Breath last night. By now, all the people inside the school have had their first dose of the mind-altering drug."

Frank quietly checked on Tim and thought he was sound asleep. 'He'll be out for a couple of hours at least.' he thought and went to the bathroom and counted Tim's medication. 'Perfect,' he thought. 'This kid isn't going to know what hit him. In a few days, his will is ours.'

He left the apartment and walked to the war room at the other end of the top floor. He knocked on the door to Sims' office.

###

Tim laid still in his bed and waited for the door to close. He heard the click. Throwing the covers back, he slowly got out of bed, his heart racing with fear.

Moving to the living room like a person searching for an intruder, Tim approached the front door. Hesitating, he put his hand on the doorknob and turned it.

The door opened, and there was no one in the hallway. Relieved, Tim returned to his bedroom and rummaged through the closet for some old running gear.

He had no idea how long Frank would be gone, but he had to try to find someone who could give him answers to his disturbing questions.

Locating a box in the back of his closet, he pulled out an old pair of blue jeans along with a dark blue polo shirt, black sneakers, and a navy-blue hoody that zipped down the front.

It felt like it took hours because of his headache and shaking from the last dose of morphine he received downstairs, but Tim got dressed.

He walked into the bathroom and brushed his teeth, thinking afterward that maybe his toothpaste had a drug in it too.

'You are paranoid, Tim!' He thought. 'I can do this; I am Isaiah's, right-hand man. No one will say anything to me.'

The front door opened. Tim's heart dropped. Frank had returned because he had left his car keys on the kitchen counter. Tim threw his sneakers behind the bed, jumped back under the covers, and covered his head. He could hear footsteps on the hardwood floor approaching the bedroom.

His heart pounded and felt like it could come out of his mouth. He forced himself to breathe slowly. If discovered, he didn't know what would happen. He would not be able to explain being fully dressed, and under his covers.

Frank peered through the door and watched the body shape heave slowly up and down. "Good boy Tim, you go ahead and sleep your life away," he said.

"You're going to be asleep for hours on that drug, so I can take my time coming back here."

Frank didn't know he just told Timothy Grayson that he was being drugged by the High Council, and Frank wouldn't be back for hours.

The footsteps moved back across the living room and out the front door. A massive sigh of relief escaped Tim's lungs.

Now he had to find out the truth and their hidden agenda that Sims was orchestrating for the High Council. He waited for ten minutes to ensure Frank wouldn't return.

He decided to move to the living room couch and sit there for a while. If anyone did come in, it would seem normal.

After Frank's visit, he got up and walked to the front door. He opened it and walked into the hall. Leaving his door unlocked, he walked toward the back stairs.

Tim cautiously walked downstairs to the main level of the school. He opened the door to the outside and walked out. His eyes did not hurt as Isaiah had told him. Tim saw a small group of people standing and praying on the other side of the perimeter fence.

He pulled the hood over his head and zipped up the jacket. Looking like one of the children, people from the buses, he walked casually toward the back fence.

Ramone looked up and saw a figure in dark clothing approach and asked,

"Can I help you, son?"

"Dude! Aren't you that Grayson guy, Mr. Sims' right-hand man?" asked Doc, both shocked and distressed.

"I thought I was." he began. "I was having migraines, and Sims gave me a pain pill, and the next thing I knew, I was recovering from brain surgery; or so he said."

"What are you doing out here and dressed like that?"

"I'm not stupid… I know something is going on."

Chapter 33: *Worried*

John ate his dinner without noticing the flavors of the food. Was his mind on an instant replay of the nightmare he had or was it a nightmare? Did David have a major medical trauma causing him to have a near-death experience?

It's not uncommon in the medical profession for patients to have an out-of-body experience stating that they could look back on themselves lying in their bed or on the operating table.

'It doesn't make sense. I was witnessing David's near-death experience!' he thought repeatedly. 'How could that happen?'

"Did you enjoy your meal?" asked the flight attendant.

"Would you like something else? I can bring you another meal."

"No, it's fine."

"Sir, you barely touched it. Was there something wrong with the meal?"

"No, of course not," he replied. "It's… my brother is missing."

"I understand sir. What's his name? I'll say a prayer for him."

"Thank you; his name is David," John replied. "I could use more coffee."

"Coming right up." He replied and took the tray back to the galley. He pulled the curtain and knelt to pray.

"Father, this one is hard-headed. He is questioning your vision you gave him. I told him I would pray for David, and though I already know you have him safe; I'll still honor John's request." The attendant stayed behind the curtain until his glow was gone and returned to John with more coffee.

"Rest easy, John. Your brother is safe." said the attendant, and he walked away.

"John! John! Wake up!" said Jason.

"Where did he go?" asked John. "The flight attendant."

"He hasn't been on deck for hours; why?"

"He just gave me my coffee and…

"And you had another dream," said Jason. "David missing has got you scared."

John looked at his empty coffee cup and called the attendant. The young man made his way to John's seat.

"Can I get you something?" he asked John and winked.

"Coffee," he replied and sat back bewildered.

The other men in the cabin were stirring awake, and the sound of the engines winding down let everyone know that an altitude change was imminent. They were less than an hour outside of Santa Fe Regional Airport.

"This is the last call for drinks as we will be landing in Santa Fe Regional Airport in approximately fifty minutes."

"Are you going to tell us about your second dream, John?" asked Baker.

"I'm not sure what it was. I was finishing dinner thinking about the first dream I had. The flight attendant asked me if everything was okay with my meal because I barely touched it. I told him about David, and he asked his name to pray for him.

I told him, and he disappeared behind the curtain to the galley.

A few minutes later, he came back and said, "Rest easy, John, your brother is safe." I guess that's when you woke me. But the guy in my dream was our attendant!"

"John. We didn't get dinner, old buddy."

The flight attendant moved through the cabin, picked up the empty cups, and returned to the galley. The captain came on the intercom.

"Gentlemen, we are ten minutes away from touch down. Please make sure your seats are upright, and your serving trays are locked and secured in place."

The rest of the team belted in and anxiously waited to disembark and meet the ground support. Flight 873 would land ahead of the Army convoy by forty minutes.

Two miles out, and everyone felt the landing gear dropdown. It was a smooth landing and the bird taxied to a plane terminal often used by the military.

The plane came to a stop, and the engines died. After a few minutes to depressurize the craft, the flight attendant opened the door. John hung back so he could exit the plane last.

"Thank you," the attendant said, "John, believe the vision God gave you. He cannot lie, and His words are trustworthy and true. David is safe."

The attendant's angelic glow returned and what John witnessed stunned him as the attendant winked again and disappeared.

John ran down the ramp to where Jason and Andre were standing. "He's an angel!" John said.

"He told me, 'Believe the vision God gave you. He cannot lie, and His words are trustworthy and true. David is safe.' Then he disappeared! I never told him about my dream!"

Chapter 34: *Returned*

David stood in the presence of pure holiness. His knees buckled and like John on the island of Patmos, he, too, fell on his face like a dead man. The Holy Spirit touched him, and his strength returned.

"Do you know why you are here, David?" asked the Holy Spirit.

"Is it my time?"

"You are here to witness events in the extremely near future. We are in a battle for the human race!"

David was distracted by the intense beauty of heaven. Colors he had only guessed at, in a garden so profoundly beautiful that one could weep at its intenseness.

He looked around him and saw angelic beings dashing to their assigned humans and countries, assuming a defensive posture. Every being was powerful, equipped with a sword and the Word of God. They had been battle-ready for eons.

David felt the presence of Almighty God surround his being. Jesus stood before him. He knelt and worshiped and honored Him.

"I have brought you here to see the dark forces on earth are ever-present in the heavenly realms as well."

"You have followed me since childhood, and I wanted to prepare you for the coming battles that are about to ensue."

"Lord, what can I do?' he asked. "I am but a man."

"My brother, our Father, knew you before the foundation of the world. You are here for such a time as this. Moses thought the same way, but My Father led Israel by him out of Egypt with His mighty hand.

Remember, all things are impossible with you, but with God, all things are possible."

David was back in his body in the infirmary. He opened his eyes, and no one was there. He felt his strength return and climbed out of bed and got dressed.

He was no longer hooked up to monitors. And the tubes in him were removed by the Holy Spirit. There was no trace of the sedative in his system.

"Lord, what did you mean by the battle about to ensue? Please show me."

Instantly David's mind filled with images of the high school. He felt a deep sense of compassion and urgency for them. The devil's breath experiment was underway, and there was a window of just a few days before everyone inside would succumb to the insidious side effects of the drug.

Old Billy and the others moved to the terrace and had settled in with coffee while discussing their plans. It was apparent that those inside the schoolhouse were in grave danger.

If carried out to fruition, their memory of loved ones, friends, and even their bank accounts is history. And there would be no memory of their past life. It was like wiping their memory clean and new ones introduced.

"It is a volatile situation. This drug is so dangerous that any evil force could use it and obliterate a person's entire life. What's worse is that it can also cause brain damage and death."

"I remember reading about Scopolamine in college. It's a member of the henbane family of poisons. It grows wild and is easily obtainable." Gennicy said.

"A victim ingests it; the person often wakes up in a park not knowing what happened or how they got there. And there is nothing they can do because when the drug wears off, usually four or five days later, the toxicology screen is useless; the drug is already out of their system."

"Billy, are you thinking that it is one way to make people accept the mark of the beast? What about free will.?"

"I don't know, Tracy, but I do know this. For decades, drug companies have convinced doctors that drugs are the answer to treating patients.

At the turn of the twentieth century, physicians also used prayer as a part of their patient's recovery.

"Globally, the legalized use of narcotics has become a recreational avenue like alcohol and cigarettes. No wonder it is so easy to introduce another drug," said Jeffery.

The five of them sat pondering the next course of action when Billy's cell phone rang.

"Hello…Yes… Okay, will do. Thanks for the update." Billy hung up.

"That was my pastor. He said that Devil's Breath is in the school people's diets. His wife Susan did a toxicology test on some donuts that an occupant secretly took from the school and handed it off to him. It is Scopolamine."

"What do we do now?" asked Jerry. "We can't just break them out of there. The people think that there was an anthrax attack and immunized against it."

"Wait a minute, what anthrax attack?" asked Gennicy.

"I just arrived and didn't know anything about any so-called anthrax attack."

"It happened a few days ago. One of the men from inside the school approached Pastor Ramone and showed him the mark on his right hand at the injection site.

It is a biomedical chip which will disappear in a few more days."

"Daddy, are you talking about Uncle Carlos?"

"Yes, honey. Uncle Carlos and the other church members have been at the high school since all this began, praying and asking for deliverance for the people trapped inside."

"What do you mean trapped? Can't they walk out the same gate they entered?"

"They could, but being drugged and spoon-fed the many lies, they have no desire to leave."

"Well," Tracy said, "we have to do something and quickly!"

"Right now, all we can do is pray. God will show us what to do. I need to head back to the school, meet up with Carlos, and find out if he has heard anything from a national level. I'm sure the rest of the world thinks that we are in a war zone and that there are countless casualties."

"Okay, I'll stay back here and take care of David."

Billy kissed his daughter on the cheek. He and Jerry went through the gun shop and climbed into the jeep parked in front of the store.

Shortly, they arrived in front of the school and found Ramone and a few others at the back gate praying. They walked up to the small group and joined the prayer with the others.

"In Jesus name, Amen." said Ramone.

"Billy, I'm glad you're here. A man by the name of Doc has been coming out, and he is the one who smuggled the donuts out to me."

"Any more contact with him?"

"It was this morning before 8:00 a.m. That's when I gave Doc the information regarding the food's toxicity results.

"I also gave him enough water and sandwiches for him and his family, so they wouldn't have to eat the food inside."

"Do you think he is going to accept Jesus?" asked Billy.

"I hope so. Doc is terrified and angry. He was a medic in the military and knew how to recognize someone's posture on drugs. He is desperate to get his family out of there!"

"Carlos, what can we do to help?"

"It's good to see you, Jerry, but right now, I think that prayer is our only source of power to fight the enemy.

Billy, I also heard that there is a medical team on the way from Fort Lewis, Washington.

The military has stepped up protocols to ensure medical relief for all the casualties. The news reports say that the convoy should arrive sometime today."

Billy's phone chirped, and he saw a message from Gennicy; it read 9-1-1!

"Something's wrong, Carlos! We have to go!"

Billy and Jerry ran to the jeep. Billy hurried across the mountain road and squealed to a stop in front of the store. They ran down to the common room and saw Gennicy terrified.

"I went to the infirmary. Daddy, David is gone!" she cried.

Chapter 35: *Faking It*

It was 3:50 p.m., and Timothy slept through his alarm. He heard the key in the front room door. Quickly he slipped into the bathroom and locked the door behind him. Frank unlocked Tim's front door and walked in. He went to the bedroom, saw the empty bed, and turned to the bathroom.

"Tim, are you in the bathroom? Is everything okay?"

"I'll be out in a minute."

He conspicuously opened the cap on his prescription bottle, threw a pill in the toilet, and flushed. He put the bottle back into the medicine cabinet.

"I need some water!" he yelled as he walked into the living room, pretending he had a pill dissolving in his mouth. Frank brought him a glass of tap water. Tim chugged half of it and cringed. "Those pills taste nasty!"

"I know they do. It's good to see that you are on top of taking your medication; no matter how bad the pills taste, they'll help you recover quicker."

"I know, but it seems that my recovery is not happening soon enough."

"It's only been a few days. Most people don't even get out of the hospital as early as you did. Give yourself some time, okay?"

"I know; it's just frustrating."

Tim sat down on the sofa and switched on the television. It was on the same floor as the war room, so the satellite feed was uninterrupted. He channel-surfed and stopped at a wildlife show and turned up the volume.

Frank went into the kitchen and prepared a snack for Tim. He brought it to him, and while Tim ate his nachos and drank a coke, Frank went into the bathroom and locked the door. He took Tim's meds from the cabinet and counted out the remaining pills. Satisfied, he returned to the living room.

An hour had passed, and Tim knew he had to act tired. He rubbed his eyes and bent his head down. "I hate the way those pills make me feel."

"You are taking strong medication, Tim. Isn't it better than hurting?"

"I think I'm going to watch TV in the bedroom so I can lay down." Tim got up from the couch and stumbled so Frank could steady him. The act was convincing enough for Frank to help Tim back to bed.

So far, Frank didn't know he was not taking his prescription and helped Tim into bed and handed him the remote control to his television.

There was a knock at the door, and Frank left to answer it and knew it was Sims waiting to receive an update.

"Is that you, Isaiah?" Tim called out.

"I'm here, Timothy. How are you feeling?"

"Groggy. Hey, thanks for hiring Frank; he has been a real-life saver helping me get around."

"I'm glad you are happy with Frank. Get some rest, and I'll see you tomorrow."

"Thanks, Isaiah, for everything."

The two left Tim's room and talked in the living room. Tim purposely dropped the remote onto the hardwood floor, and Frank and Isaiah went back to Tim's bedroom.

He cocked his head slightly to the left and allowed his left hand to dangle over the bed toward the floor. Spittle drooled down his mouth.

Frank picked up the remote, turned the TV off, and set the remote on the nightstand. He took Tim's left hand, placed it under the covers, grabbed a tissue, and wiped Tim's chin. Frank and Sims walked out of the room, leaving the door open.

"You almost convinced me that you are a caregiver," said Sims grinning. "Grayson doesn't even know what your true vocation is."

"For now, anyway. Tim is taking the pills on schedule. He almost choked on his afternoon dose."

"He'll be asleep for the next six hours; why don't you come to my place for dinner?

Four days from now, Timothy Grayson's free will is a thing of the past.

Tuesday, I want a blood draw from him to find out his levels." Sims said and closed the front door.

Chapter 36: *Hostile*

Colonel Baker, Jason, and David returned to the cabin, and there was no flight attendant on board. The three sat down and tried to assess the situation. The captain came out of the cockpit.

"Is everything okay, colonel? This bird is in bed for the night, so if you need it for a private meeting?"

"We'll be out of here in a few minutes, thank you." The captain nodded, placed his hat on his head, and left.

They looked at each other.

"I don't know what's happening here, but it has to be God orchestrating it. How else could the weather delay our flight by three days?"

"The weird weather we flew through and being diverted to Santa Fe. All of it is way beyond coincidence. What do you think, dad?"

"I never thought I'd see so many obstacles fall right into place at just the right time. A few years back, before old Billy retired, he and Shelley led your mom and me to Christ.

Otherwise, I would have thought John was a nut case. So, I agree, God has designed this entire scenario."

"What's next?" asked John as they exited the plane.

The three caught up with the rest of the team in baggage and retrieved theirs. Outside was a shuttle to take the team to the airport's central part, where the convoy would meet them. It was located at a gate on the south end of the field, away from civilian traffic. The terminal's lights were on, and vending machines lined the walls inside the door. Everyone walked in and found a place to sit.

"Gentleman," said the colonel, "as you were." The team sat back down.

"Gentlemen, as you know, the area we are heading into has many unknowns. Treat it like a hostile environment.

It won't be the locals we have to worry about but the bombs. The convoy arriving soon also has bomb techs who will help locate the unexploded devices.

Once we enter the hot zone, we'll need to set up triage and an emergency tent to treat the wounded and evac them out of the area."

"Sir? How will we know where to set up the medical tents and ours, especially with the bombs going off and no one knows where they are at?"

"After World War II, the military set up stockpiles of the unused devices across the United States; most of them were underground. There are records as to their locations, and with the help of satellite telemetry, it should pinpoint the disposal sites.

"Hold tight until the convoy arrives. But don't leave the area. I suggest you get a little more shut-eye if possible."

###

"Well," said Jason, "Technology has finally caught up to vending machines. You can now swipe your debit/credit card and buy a candy bar for a buck-fifty and be charged an additional fifty cents for using your card."

Baker moved to the coffee machine and dropped a dollar in quarters into the slot.

The cup slid down, and the black syrup mixed with the hot water and filled the cup. He removed it and took a drink.

"Just like the army brew, thick and bitter." He said and laughed. "Some things never change. Twenty years ago, the coffee from machines was bad. Their recipe has not changed!"

Ten minutes later, four jeeps and five duce-and-a-half trucks and a water truck pulled up to the terminal. The tactical support team had arrived, and the men and women in convoy stretched their legs and some lit-up smokes.

All of them were in full combat gear. The four-and-a-half-hour ride in army vehicles from the base was not comfortable.

The commanding officer was Colonel Chase Saunders. He climbed from the first jeep and walked into the terminal. His sergeant yelled, "Ten Hut!"

Everyone inside scrambled to attention. Salutes and handshakes showed proper military protocols.

"Sandy, I didn't know you're at White Sands."

"Andre, it's good to see you. Sorry, it's because of emergency circumstances."

"You remember my son-in-law, Jason Roberts. And this is Jason's childhood friend John Garner."

"Pleased to meet you, sir."

"It's a pleasure. And it's Sandy. You are also a doctor?"

"Yes, I volunteered to come on this mission because my brother David moved to Albuquerque a few days ago, just before the bombs began exploding. Colonel Baker was kind enough to allow me to tag along."

"Glad to have you. We have no idea how many causalities we will encounter, and we also experienced some unusual weather driving here from White Sands. Rain, lightning, thunder, and hail. And it felt like it was following us."

"I know what you mean! We had our share of rough weather while airborne. I can't explain it either." Andrea said.

For the next hour, Baker and Saunders went over travel plans and protocols necessary to accomplish their mission.

More salutes and handshakes and the team climbed into the jeeps, and the rest of the troops boarded. Fifty-eight minutes away from Albuquerque and John replayed the events on the plane.

The plane ride was like a boat in a perfect storm. The dreams and meeting an honest to God angel were more than John could wrap his head around.

Now each jar, each bump from the jeep ride jerked John back into the present, and he realized everything was happening, and none of it was a dream.

Five miles out, it began to rain again. All the trucks had their canvas tops on so the rain wouldn't be a problem.

Saunders and Baker road in the first jeep, and John and Jason took the second one in line. If needed, they could communicate with each other through the walkie-talkies carried in the vehicles.

As the convoy traveled north on Old Highway 25, the rain increased, and the wind blew heavy gusts against the vehicles' sides.

The sky lit up as lightning trailed across the horizon. Rumbling thunder shouted in the air, roaring, and making it hard to hear each other's voices.

Hail the size of marbles pelted the convoy. Saunders ordered the convoy to stop.

"We need to find cover! The canvas won't out last this hail." His Sergeant got on the squawk box and instructed the convoy to pay close attention to any shelter away from the storm.

One of the convoy men knew the area and relayed to the colonel about an abandoned airplane hangar a couple of clicks from their position just up the road. They found the old airport and pulled the convoy inside a giant hangar a jet could fit in. There they would wait out the storm.

John was more frustrated. It was one delay after another. The team is safe in the hanger for now.

John climbed out of the jeep and walked to the front of the open hangar. The hail was coming down and bouncing on the old tarmac like ping pong balls.

'What do you want from me, God?' John thought. 'Is this punishment for treating my kid brother so rough when we were growing up?'

'Mr. Take Charge isn't in charge anymore. God is.' He thought and returned to the jeep.

It was three-forty-five p.m. central mountain time, late afternoon, and he was no closer to finding his brother. He felt helpless.

###

Both ends of the hangar were open and had no doors. Their arrival due to the storm had left them tired, cold, and hungry.

The colonel ordered potbellied stoves to be set up inside by the hangar openings to fend off some of the cold. A large propane stove heated, and the cook began making the evening meal.

John was annoyed and asked, "Colonel, are we going to camp out here, or are we going to advance to the hot zone?"

"Doctor! We have been here going on three hours now, and the weather hasn't let up except for the wind. Everyone on this team feels like you do! They are just as tired and frustrated as you are! What's more, they are all hungry!"

"Sorry, sir. I'm aching to find my brother."

"John, I know you are, and we all have vested interests in going. But it doesn't help to be negative and voicing what everyone else is thinking but can't say."

"Forgive me, colonel, you're right; I shouldn't have said anything."

"You're forgiven. We haven't eaten for hours, and to be effective once we do get there, we need to take care of ourselves first."

"You're right." John felt foolish because he wasn't looking at the bigger picture.

The cook opened several gallon cans of beef stew and heated two pots to feed the immense crew.

The temporary shelter warmed up from the two heaters. Hot coffee circulated fast, and the chow line grew and diminished as each soldier received food.

Cots were brought out and used as makeshift chairs. Most utensils, bowls, and napkins were disposable and made for quick cleanup and quick exits.

Jason, Andre, and John shared a cot and ate their stew. John said out loud what Baker and the rest of his team were feeling. He envied him for such latitude.

A sergeant walked over to colonel Baker and saluted.

"Sorry to interrupt you, sir; I've just received word that the storm is going to last well into the early morning hours."

"Thank you, sergeant. Listen up! Dig in and get some sleep. We are stuck here till morning. As you were!"

The military team gave Colonel Baker a salute and set up cots and sleeping bags.

The jeeps and duce-and-a-half trucks did not leave much room for sleeping outside of them. A few soldiers chose the floor, and the rest of the enlisted personnel retreated to the trucks. They found enough room for the officers to bunk on cots.

The hours ebbed. The tin roof was pummeled relentlessly by the marble-sized hail. It stopped to regain strength and started again. Dozing off was sporadic.

The pounding of the rain was also loud and unforgiving. Lightning streaked across the horizon as if chasing an invisible target.

Thunder exploded overhead and made sure that no one in the old hanger would embrace sleep. Exhaustion forced many to shut down their senses rather than rest. The final insult was the roof leaking in several areas, which seemed to target the army cots.

Tonight, the elements won.

"I'm getting too old for this kind of abuse," whispered Baker. Both turned and saw the dripping water from the roof, hitting the colonel's sleeping bag.

"Looks like Chinese water torture to me, dad," said Jason, with a slight giggle.

"You are full of charm tonight. Do you want to trade bunks, soldier?" Baker snickered. "I'll move it a few inches closer to both of you, and it will miss me."

Baker sat up and heard a distinct rattling sound.

"Don't move!" yelled Saunders.

"Turn your flashlights onto the floor. Everyone searched the hangar floor with flashlights and saw several southeastern Diamondback rattlesnakes coiled in an attack posture.

"Everyone! Stay where you are, and don't make any sudden moves! These are some bad boys, and we don't have any antivenom serum with us. Turn the headlights on." He slowly stepped down onto the concrete.

Saunders grew up in Arizona and was familiar with rattlesnakes. The southeastern Diamondbacks were awful news because they were the rattlesnake's most venomous species.

Chapter 37: *Astonished*

Are you looking for me?" David asked as he walked from his bedroom.

"David! What are you doing upstairs and out of the infirmary?"

Gennicy ran and leaped into his arms, crying. He held her, and the two were motionless.

"Don't scare me like that!" she complained and gently punched his arm in mock anger.

The entire team crowded around him, giving him hugs and looks of astonishment.

"I'm famished!" David said. "The food smells great. I'm okay, Genn Stop fussing."

He sat down, and all eyes focused on David, waiting for the explanation as to why he recovered so quickly. He took a bite of his sandwich and sipped on his coffee.

"I don't know where to begin…" he said and took another bite of his tuna sandwich.

"Maybe this will help. This afternoon Jerry and I went to the high school and spoke with Carlos Ramone, my pastor. There have been some remarkable developments at the school since we were there."

Everyone sat drinking their coffee and listened while Billy told them that the schoolhouse was under demonic attack. The use of a drug is inside the food. And confirmed his suspicions regarding the darkness connected to the school.

He also shared with the others about a man named Doc, who knows, the school's people are being drugged. He smuggled donuts out to Carlos for toxins screening. Carlos is also giving untainted food and water to Doc and his family. With that said, you scared us! How did you get out of your bed?

"Billy, You forgot to tell them about the military convoy on the way with doctors and medical supplies," said Jerry. David's bottom jaw dropped.

"From where?" he asked excitedly.

"Fort Lewis, Washington. Why?"

"Jason Roberts is at Fort Lewis, and if I know my brother, he contacted Jason so he could tag along."

Billy nodded and sipped his coffee.

"So, what happened, David?" asked Billy.

There was an urgency in his voice, and David could tell that there was more going on than he had shared. He finished the last couple of swallows of his tomato soup.

"My spirit was taken away, by the Holy Spirit." He replied. This time was different than the others." He paused.

"He took me to heaven."

Chapter 38: *Set Up!*

"What are you talking about, Mr. Grayson?" asked Ramone.

"It's Tim, and I'm talking about being used as a test subject with a drug that removes free will and without my knowledge! I want to know the truth! And I know I won't get it from Sims."

A guard walked toward the three, and each quickly moved away from the other.

"I'll keep you updated.

Sims is drugging the people inside, including my family. You can find me in the main housing; I'm Doc."

"Right," said Tim and walked away.

Ramone and the other Christians began to pray for the people inside and Tim and Doc as they went back into the building.

Tim made his way back to his apartment, unnoticed. He changed back into his pajamas and crawled into bed. Maybe he's safe for now, but he wasn't sure for how long.

It was 9:00 a. m., and now he was feeling tired, but he remembered he had to put back the clothes he wore and his sneakers. The closet was always a mess, so that wasn't a problem.

He set his cell phone alarm for 3:45 p.m. so he could dispose of another pill.

He crawled back into bed and eventually drifted off to sleep without the help of drugs.

"Okay, I'll talk to you later… uh huh... Frank is here…" said Sims and hung up the landline.

"Come in, Frank. How is our test subject doing?"

"He is drugged, boss, and asleep," Frank laughed.

"Great idea making him your right hand man. Setting that kid up was brilliant!"

"Brilliant only if it works. Did you count Tim's meds?"

"Yeah, and he hasn't skipped any doses. I don't think he suspects a thing."

"That's good news but see to it that he stays on the prescribed regimen."

"Will do boss, Tim is going to be out for hours, so I need a few things from my apartment, and I'll be back before his next dose is due."

"Do what you need to, and I'll talk to you later."

"I don't think I'll need to spike his food. He is too willing to take his meds. Touch base with you later."

He left Sims' office feeling smug and essential.

"Damon, I just spoke with Frank, and Grayson doesn't know anything. He is all too willing to take his medication.

"No, I know. A blood draw will be taken from Tim in three or four days to measure how much of his free will is gone. Okay, I'll call you in a few days, so let the High Council know what is happening and that everything is moving forward as planned."

Sims hung up and lit a cigarette. The cocaine bolstered his enormous ego higher.

'Humans will be easy to destroy.' said his demon.

Chapter 39: *The Future*

David could not fathom that he was in the presence of Jesus. He knelt before him, not knowing what else to do. His spirit bathed in pure holiness; he drank in the peace and joy that enveloped him. Jesus bent down, took David's hand, raised him to his feet, and kissed his forehead.

"I've been waiting for this moment. I've loved you when the world was a mere thought. Before time became time, I knew you when you first appeared in my heart and when you would accept me as your Lord and Savior. I know when you will come home to me and all the marvelous things you will accomplish in my name before then."

David walked with Jesus and listened to every word. He longed to stay with him forever from that moment. They walked in the garden in all its splendor, but the garden paled to the majesty of Jesus.

Neither spoke, but somehow David knew everything and didn't need answers to anything. The mysteries of heaven were shown to him by the Lord.

They stopped, and David spoke.

"Lord, will I remember everything? It's all so overwhelming; the past, the present, and the future is so clear to me and what must take place."

"You will remember what you need to for the advancement of the kingdom." Jesus said and smiled.

"The peace and the joy I give you will remain in you, but not some of the future events. There is no reason for you to know anything other than the events that will affect you and the others."

Jesus looked at the Holy Spirit as the Lord sauntered away. We watched until He disappeared into the garden. David felt himself traveling downward back into his body.

"That's when I got out of bed and got dressed. The Holy Spirit freed me from my entrapments and the morphine." David said and sipped his coffee.

"Billy, Does the name Colonel Baker mean anything to you?"

"He's my old best friend from school. Why do you ask?"

"He is on his way here."

"Jesus must have told you a lot of things. Is Jason with him as well?"

"Yes, as is my brother. The Lord told me they were safe and in Santa Fe. They won't get here for a while. He also told me that obstacles were placed to delay their arrival so they would arrive at the right time."

"I don't quite understand that bit of information, but John will probably tell me when they get here." he said finished his coffee.

"What was it like?" asked Tracy, excited.

"It was almost surreal. Standing in the presence of pure holiness would have destroyed our bodies but our spirit drinks in the experience.

The colors in heaven are so beautiful but dim next to the splendor of Christ. Your heart fills with such overflowing love that you feel ready to burst; instead, you revel in the pure joy of it."

"I cannot wait!" said Jerry. "Did Jesus say anything about any of us? Was there a special message for anyone in particular?"

David shook his head no.

"It's incredible, I knew everything from beginning to end about our lifetime on earth, but when I returned, I can only remember what is happening and what is about to take place."

"What can you tell us about what is happening?" I've been feeling a sense of urgency about the high school and its occupants." asked Billy.

"Me too," said Jerry, "and I think something devastating is about to happen." The others agreed with Jerry and were anxious to hear what David experienced.

"Your visit to the school, Billy, was God's timing. There are now key players on the inside that will orchestrate God's plan to destroy the evil plot against the people.

The high school is a test run to establish a global attack on humankind's will. Satan has devised an insidious test to rob people of their free will. That is what Scopolamine does to the mind."

"I understand the use of the drug in larger doses renders its victim to auto-suggestions and can erase their recent memory.

While in the military, experiments were done on a much smaller scale and controlled.

The military wanted to see the implications of such a drug. The volunteers received simple suggestions forgetting what they ate that day or their first pet's name. It all seemed innocent at first." said Billy.

"I'll be right back. I just received a message coming in from a satellite transmission."

He left the common room and went to the communication center located on the floor below them. Jerry keyed in his password, and the National Weather Service flashed on his screen.

'What's going on?' he thought. 'I'm not tied into this link.'

He hit escape and redirected the com to the local news. Most releases told the readers about the sensational updates on the world war II bombs and how they were suddenly quiet and no longer a threat. Still, the news warned the residents in and around Albuquerque, New Mexico, to be alert for the possibility of more explosions. The weather was responsible for the reprieve, bringing its cooler temperatures.

While the others waited for Jerry's return, the group chatted about the events leading up to where they were. Gennicy sat next to David, holding his hand. Jeffery and Tracy excused themselves and headed to the kitchen to prepare dinner.

The evening meal would be quick to prepare. Jeffery had pre-baked potatoes, a garden salad prepped, fresh broccoli, and a dessert he had made just after breakfast.

New York steak broiled to perfection would take but minutes to prepare.

Tracy went about setting the table for the six of them. She brewed more coffee. Everything was ready except for the steaks. Each steak was cooked to order, according to personal preference.

Jerry was about to leave when the National Weather Service popped up on the monitor again. He decided to open it. He couldn't believe the report and printed a copy and headed upstairs.

The others had returned to the dinner table when Jerry entered. He sat down and handed the report to Billy.

“Is this real?” he asked. “What’s your source?”

“The National Weather Service.”

“This area is not known for tornados!”

“What?!” gasped the others.

“There must be a mistake, Jerry.”

“Wait a minute, Billy.” said David.

“God can bring any natural disaster on the world if he wants to. It’s a ploy God uses to disrupt the enemy's plans. God just gave me a word of knowledge. We are to wait on him. Do nothing and trust him.”

“What are we supposed to do?” asked Gennicy. “How can we sit back and do nothing?”

“Because God removes all possible means of fixing the situation to make way for a miracle. I am going to do something, give thanks for dinner and eat.”

“Well,” said Jerry. “In the mid-twentieth century, the warning time was a few minutes. Now in 2019, the warning time is closer to half an hour.”

“That’s comforting!” said Billy.

“Hey, old friend, the last tornado that touched down in Albuquerque back in 2007 and was an EF2. Which means that the wind velocity was 125 mph and was twelve years ago.”

“David is right. God can do what he wants to. Now that the warning system has improved, the tornado could dissipate before it ever makes contact. Remember, God is in control.” said Jerry.

Jeffery returned to the kitchen with the orders and prepared everyone’s steak to their liking. Tracy served them as they came from the broiler. Most wanted medium-rare, so it did not take long to prepare them. Tracy and Jeffery fixed theirs and joined the others.

"You're also right, Jerry. It's the year 2019 and not the dark ages." said Billy. "David, would you like to say grace?"

"Yes." he said. Everyone closed their eyes, folded their hands, and bowed their heads, but David looked up toward heaven.

"Thank you, Lord, for taking care of your children and letting us know you are always in control. Thank you for the rich bounty of food you have given us. Bless it and keep us healthy, so we may continue to do your will. In Jesus name, Amen."

Everyone enjoyed their dinner and moved to the balcony to discuss protocols for the impending tornado.

No one knew that the morning would bring the unexpected.

Chapter 40: *Security*

Frank rinsed the dirty dishes and cleaned the rest of the apartment. He checked on Tim numerous times and saw that he was still sleeping, or so he thought.

Tim changed his position in bed to indicate a sleep pattern. After the place was spotless, Frank left and headed to Isaiah's apartment next to the war room.

Frank knocked on Isaiah's door, and a valet opened it and showed him in. He offered him a mixed drink, and he joined his boss at the dining room table.

"This whisky sour is great." he said and threw a swallow to the back of his throat.

"Next drink straight up. And make it Scotch."

"Tim will be out till 10:00 p.m., and he will be up to take a pill at that time."

"How can, you be sure?"

"He was choking on a pill this afternoon and was yelling for water. He commented on the foul taste, and I reminded him that it was better not to be in pain. He agreed." Frank tossed the shot of Scotch down his throat.

"Excellent. Just keep counting those pills. I don't think you'll have to babysit Tim through the night. It sounds like he is doing the work for us. Now, I have a special treat for you tonight, flown in this morning from Maine."

The waiter served two plates of filet mignon and lobster tails with clarified butter. A basket of hot dinner rolls sat on the table, and the drinks switched from hard liquor to a merlot. A baked potato with the works graced the two entrees. They raised their wine glasses and toasted the perfect meal.

"Bona petit," said the waiter and left the room.

Isaiah and Frank relished every butter-drenched bite of lobster and steak. The dinner rolls sopped up the butter and the steak's juices and the sour cream from the baked potato.

Sipping the wine was a pleasure rinsing the pallet getting it ready for dessert. New York cheesecake with strawberries and chocolate ran down the sides, topped off the extraordinary meal.

"You sure know how to entertain, boss." said Frank as he licked the saucer clean from all the richness left behind.

"I've got connections." he replied, his demon boasted.

"That's what I like about you, Frank; you don't care what anyone thinks." said Sims as he lapped up the flavors from his cheesecake as well.

"Who cares about what people think! After those bonehead Christians are gone, we can finally do whatever we want!"

"Exactly! The ones left behind are like dumb animals and will believe whatever we tell them. Who knows, maybe UFOs took them away." he laughed with demonic amusement.

The waiter removed the plates from the table and brought each a mirror with two thin white powder lines with straws.

The men put their straws into their nostrils and sniffed as they guided the straw down the disappearing line.

The other line soon vanished in the opposite nostril, and both relaxed back into their chairs as the cocaine flooded their bloodstream.

"Now this is the real dessert!" said Frank. Isaiah nodded.

###

It was 6:00 p.m., and Doc wondered about Tim and if he was doing okay. Jane and the kids were getting ready to go to dinner, but Doc had set out more PB &J's and bottled water for him and his family.

They were so hungry that none questioned how he had gotten so many sandwiches and bottled waters.

"Honey," that was so thoughtful of you to bring back food for us while we slept." said Jane and she took a bite of her sandwich.

"I have your backs, right. I couldn't let you starve."

Jane and the kids were happy to see him eating again. Maybe now, he would stop all the nonsense regarding his evil conspiracy theory of being drugged.

What did they expect? His parents were ex-hippies. His family did not realize that what he suspected was genuine and not a theory.

Seven o'clock in the morning would come quickly, and he wondered if he could safely venture out again for more food and water from Ramone. He also was worried that Tim wouldn't be able to sneak out.

"I'm still hungry."

The smell of roast beef played with her nostrils. Jane moved toward the door, and Doc blocked her. How would he explain to her that they could not go out and eat in the cafeteria?

"What are you doing?"

"Honey, wait a minute." he replied, grabbed Jane, pulled her into himself, and hugged her. He kissed her.

They held each other and Jane temporarily forgot about leaving.

"Gross, dad!"

"Wow! You haven't done that in a while."

"I'm sorry. Since everything has happened, I realized that I could have lost you and the kids."

"I have a great idea. Why don't we think of things we can remember when all of us spent time together having fun just hanging out?"

His family humored him but fought the urges to run out and feast on the drug-laced food. The exercise Doc had initiated was working. Their drug-fogged minds began to have more clarity. As the evening progressed, there was laughter and happiness he hadn't seen in a long time.

Soon the smell of food left, and his family forgot about going out to troll for it. The desperation of constant hunger subsided.

Doc figured out how to lock his door from the inside so someone could not enter again unannounced. His wife and kids had gone into their rooms, the kids to play video games, and Jane looked for a movie to watch. There was a soft tap at the door.

"I noticed you and your family missed dinner, so I thought you might want some, so I brought four dinners for you." said a well-meaning server, and she handed them to Doc.

"Thank you." he said and took the dinners, shut the door, and locked it. Fortunately, the meals were well sealed, and no intoxicating aromas escaped.

Now, what do I do?' he thought. He took the meals, placed them inside the bag the sandwiches were in and slipped it under his coat.

"Doc was someone at the door?" asked Jane as the kids poked their heads out of the rooms to hear what was happening.

"Security knocked, Jane." he answered. "They wanted to make sure we were fine."

"Why would they do that? They haven't done that before."

"Dude! I don't know!" he replied in an annoyed tone.

"You know I hate it when you talk hippie!" She went back to watching her movie.

It was a chick-flick, and she knew that they turned off Doc. The two kids giggled and returned to their respective video games.

Doc sat on the sofa and took a deep breath. 'Man!' he thought. 'A person could die from so many close calls!'

There was an abrupt knock on the door, and two guards overrode the lock and pulled Doc from his quarters. His family did not hear it.

"Come with us!" one said.

Doc was sure he had been caught and was about to face his death.

"What's going on!" he demanded.

The guards remained silent but proceeded to the top floor and Tim's apartment. One opened the door, and both pushed Doc through it and left.

Chapter 41: *Snakes*

Saunders knew How to catch poisonous snakes. He carefully looked for a hook he could use to capture them and return them to the desert in the morning.

"I need a count. How many are there?"

"There are seven, sir," yelled a corporal. "I know how to catch them also, sir. I want to help."

"Affirmative corporal. No one else is to move about the floor. Corporal?"

"Davis, sir…"

"No one is to be on the deck except Corporal Davis and me until you hear an all-clear. Understood?"

A loud "Yes, sir!" resonated inside the hangar. The snakes rattled their warnings because of the loud response.

Davis and Saunders found three-foot metal poles with prongs that would serve as snake catchers.

Gunnysacks lined the walls and were there for snake control. Davis caught the first one and bagged it; twisting the top of the bag down to the bottom, he tied it off and grabbed another sack.

Saunders slid the pronged metal under the neck of a another one and moved it into a gunnysack. Two down and five to go, then the hangar would be safe again. The two moved through the hangar with stealth precision, not wanting to get bit.

Fear is the first line of defense with these creatures. Without it, one might become too confident, and results could be deadly.

Davis and Saunders had caught countless snakes growing up and knew their temperaments and how to calm them. About forty-five minutes later, Saunders and Davis safely secured all the snakes.

Saunders gave Davis a high-five, and the two took the bagged critters and placed them in the southeast part of the hangar. Still able to strike, their distance and ability was hampered.

A final sweep was done, searching under the trucks and along the inside walls, making sure the two men caught all the snakes.

"Great job, Corporal Davis! All clear!" said Saunders.

"Thank you, sir." he replied.

"How did you learn how to handle snakes?"

"I started relatively young. My brother is a herpetologist, and I used to go with him to catch snakes to milk and then release them. My brother always said,

"There is never enough venom from southeastern Diamondbacks to create antivenom."

So, he taught me how to catch them, and we doubled the amount of venom collected."

"Well done!" said Saunders. "Report to me when we return to base. I would like to explore some options with you regarding the collection of these snakes."

"Yes, sir." he said and stood at attention and saluted him."

"At ease, son. You deserve it. It can be nerve-racking catching these snakes. I forgot how frightening they are."

###

John nestled down into his sleeping bag and closed his eyes. He rehashed the visions in his mind.

Rolling to his left side, John opened his eyes and saw a brightly clad image of a man standing at the hanger entrance.

The storm still raged outside behind him. The man moved closer to John, and his glow softened.

"You!" He shouted. "You're the angel on the plane!" yelled John.

"My name is Theo and yes, I was on the plane with you to keep the plane from coming apart in the storm.

Father sent me because the enemy knew you and your team are heading to the hot zone, as you put it."

"Why all the secrecy? You could have just appeared to me on the plane instead of coming to me in dreams." John replied.

"The message was personal and intended for you, John, and not the whole crew. I am here again to give you another message from Almighty God."

John began to tremble and felt all the guilt he grew up with and was ashamed. There was no doubt that God was speaking directly to him through this angel.

"Do not fear John, for what I show you is from the Lamb of God. David calls an older man, Billy, and Billy is Colonel Baker's old school chum. They are all safe."

"The reason I came here was to show you and the others that David had been taken away by the Holy Spirit and shown many things happening at the high school.

David never suffered a stroke or was in a coma but was shown that the high school is the devil's test sight to lure people into his lair. David must see these things."

"For what purpose? I thought God was in control."

"He is, but you also live in a fractured world, and it belongs to the devil. He is the prince of the air. The leader of darkness. A shroud has been placed around the school to keep Christians out."

"David did not go inside the high school. His strong faith saved him."

"Your faith is strong also, John. But you put it to sleep for years. It is time to wake it up. In the next few days, Satan will be moving on to the high school to oppress all those trapped inside.

There are many Christians who have rallied around the school to pray for the people who innocently entered that dark realm, thinking your government controlled it."

"What you are saying is that it is only a small section outside of town that is in any danger? What is the real casualty count?"

"Yes, only a small community was hit. David had rented a condominium in that community, and his condo was destroyed. So, he thought that the U.S.A. was at war with someone. Until he met old Billy, that was his assumption."

"There is one other thing. All the delays occurred when the leaders of the forces of darkness caught wind that the military was coming.

They devised a plan called 'Operation Boom' to destroy the entire school and everyone in it.

Three bombs are ready to go off inside the school. It will wipe out all evidence of everyone in or outside the school. Had you arrived three days ago, you and the team would have died also. Because of the delays, it saved the people and your team from destruction."

"God is in control. You said there was something else. What is it?"

Theo looked up.

"Yes, Lord," he said. "Not now, John, I'll tell you later."

Theo's presence glowed, and his brightness shot straight through the roof of the hangar and was gone. John bolted awake.

Chapter 42: *The unexpected*

Breakfast rolled in early, and the smell of sausage, toast, eggs with hash browns filled the room. It was aromatherapy of breakfast foods. Carafes of coffee were sitting at the table, muffins and toast adorned the entrees. The lights went out.

"There is a malfunction in grid sixteen."

"Initiating emergency power." The lights came back on but less illuminated.

"We can still enjoy our breakfast. Jerry, eat first."

"I'm way ahead of you, Billy."

"David!" screamed Gennicy.

"Help me get him on the couch! Daddy, what is happening to him?"

The three men carried David's limp body and placed him on the sofa. Gennicy checked his eyes and said, "He's asleep. But how is that possible?"

"The Holy Spirit needs him and took him away again.

I know you're scared, but, honey, you need to trust God that he is fine, and that God will bring him back after teaching him."

"I know daddy. I know all this, but it still scares me. I've never been around anyone who has experienced such things, let alone David. He never had any of these episodes while in college. Why now?"

"Maybe it wasn't necessary until now, honey." Billy hugged his daughter.

"You are so much like your mother, so caring and loving." He kissed her forehead.

"I think the best thing we can do right now is to let David rest. They all moved back to the dining room table and ate breakfast in silence.

###

"Where am I?" asked David.

"I think there is someone here who wants to see you."

David walked along in a lush garden, not heaven but beautiful. As he walked, he could feel a familiar presence. It was also moving toward him. The two met and gasped.

"David!"

"John!"

Both embraced each other and wept uncontrollably. God instructed the Holy Spirit to bring them together. David's need to see his big brother and John's need to reconcile and forgive himself for years of guilt and shame was great.

"John, the Lord, arranged this meeting," said the Holy Spirit.

"You are entering into a battle, and you need to be focused on Jesus to succeed. Right here, right now, you need to receive the Lord's healing and forgiveness. David is here to help you."

"It's okay big brother… I love you so much."

"How! I was such a jerk to you growing up." Tears streamed down his face.

"John, I forgave you a long time ago. We were kids, and kids can be mean. Since I forgave you, you need to forgive yourself; otherwise, the enemy will have a foothold on your spiritual life."

"I guess so! But I don't know how."

"Speak from your heart John. You know what to say." said the Holy Spirit.

John knelt to pray, and David laid hands on him.

###

The others gathered and said a prayer for David.

"Daddy, how long will David be out? I mean, asleep."

"That depends on the Holy Spirit and the message God wants him to receive. When you got here, he had

been unconscious for two days. That is why we took him to the infirmary and hooked him up to I.V. fluids.

At that time, it was our first experience of him being taken away in the spirit. He told us that most of them happened while he was asleep at night."

"I hope he is okay."

"Honey, he is okay because he is with God. Have faith and trust in Him, who is doing all of this. David has given us some valuable information while in the spirit."

"I know he has." She said and hugged Billy.

###

The desert was so beautiful in the morning light, projecting her brilliant fall colors and minor skirmishes from predators chasing breakfast. Birds sang glorious love songs to their mates.

It was a majestic spectacle. The brilliant oranges, yellows, reds, and greens were displayed as each leaf surrendered its color to brown. The desert floor had a carpet of brown leaves, making it easier for prey to escape their predators.

Jerry had fitted the windows on the terrace with zoom-in capabilities that brought the desert floor closer, revealing nature's splendor. It was like being directly in front of the creatures feeling their excitement and fear.

He relished the idea of seeing God's creation up close. Everyone thrilled at witnessing the activity below the secret home. The small knit family continually gave God the praise for such splendor.

It was a cacophony of God displaying His power, glory, and presence on the earth. This pure evidence of God's existence could not be ignored. And those who believed, constantly marveled at His creation.

###

When he created the power grid program, he built a failsafe protocol if a burnt wire needed replacing. The system designs shuts down the grid automatically and reroute power through an alternate safety grid until fixed.

That way, the damage would not increase exponentially, causing a fire or worse. Three or four computer strokes and the computer announced that power grid sixteen's malfunction resolved. Satisfied, Jerry headed back upstairs.

He saw David sleeping and walked out onto the terrace and poured a cup of coffee.

"How's David?" he asked.

"He's fine," Billy replied. "He's turned over a couple of times. I bet that he'll have some exciting news to share once he wakes up. These journeys are happening more frequently."

"Daddy, I don't know what to think of all this. I am scared!

Chapter 43: *Switching Sides*

Grayson fell backward as Doc flew through the door, landing on all fours. They looked at each other in sheer panic and shock, thinking the other had initiated this dangerous meeting.

Tim quickly opened the door and peered out into the hall to see if anyone was there.

"Are you crazy coming here? How did you find my apartment? What are you doing here, anyway!

"Me! Hey man! I thought you ordered me brought here!

Two guards grabbed me out of my apartment, said nothing, but strong-armed me right to your door!"

Tim quickly shut the door and bolted it. They went into the bedroom to talk; in case anyone came through the door unannounced. Minutes passed, and Timothy went into the kitchen and brought water to Doc.

"Are you hungry?" he asked. "I overheard Frank telling Sims that he didn't have to spike my food because I am so willing to take my meds."

"Yeah, what do you got?" asked Doc. They walked into the kitchen, and Tim opened the fridge as Doc anxiously looked in.

"Here are taco fixings. Interested?"

He pulled out the bowl of taco meat and shredded cheese and pointed to the cupboard for Doc to grab the flour tortilla shells. He grabbed them, made two tacos, and placed them on a paper plate Tim handed him.

"Who do you think the two guards were that brought you here?"

"I don't know. Maybe angels." he laughed. "Do you believe in all that religious stuff?"

"Mom raised me by herself, and she was adamant regarding salvation and going to hell. So much so, she drove me away. I do think there are spiritual forces out there, somewhere, but I'm not going to discount anything, especially angels, in case she's right."

"What made you start doubting what's going on in the school?" asked Doc as he took the last bite of his second taco.

"Several things, primarily because of what my mom said.

'In the last days, people will be lovers of themselves, and the love for many will grow cold.'

I didn't understand it or cared until the High Council wanted us to blow up the school to eliminate any evidence exposing their sinister plot. There are women and children and babies in the school! I could not believe what I was hearing."

"Are you telling me that they are going to blow up the school? When?"

"At first, when they heard the U.S. Marine and Army medical contingent was on the way. Then a storm hit and delayed their arrival. I don't mind telling you, I was relieved."

"What changed their minds?"

"I did. Instead, they decided to test me, and I had no idea that I was nothing more than a pawn to be used for the High Council's hidden agenda.

Sims kept feeding me drugs he called recreational, but I think Sims gave me one to trigger my migraines."

He pulled a bottle of Oxycontin out of his desk drawer and handed it to me and convinced me that it would rid me of my headache. I finally took one.

The next thing I knew, I woke up with a headache from hell, excuse the pun, and had staples in my head. The morphine he gave me also has Scopolamine."

"Man, that's messed up!"

"When I got home, I wasn't hurting as bad and skipped a dose of the painkillers. That's when I overheard Sims telling Frank to count my pills.

So I went into the bathroom and started flushing doses. I'm a good actor because both think I'm taking my meds as prescribed. The entire scenario is so disgusting!"

Tim looked at his watch. It was 11:30 p.m. He quickly cleaned up the dishes.

"I'd better get out of here." said Doc. "We are both dead if they catch us."

Tim lit a cigarette and left it in the ashtray.

"I smoke, so I had to light up to make it look like I'm still hooked and to make them think that the drugged smoke is entering my system."

"That stinks! What is it?"

"It's a marijuana-laced cigarette."

"I'll tell you what. My parents were hippies, and I never smelled pot smell like this stuff does! That's synthetic and is no doubt addicting!"

Tim took one puff to light it and started feeling sick. Doc helped him back to the bedroom. He sat on the bed as his stomach began doing full gainers waiting to eject the contents of his stomach.

"It's 11:45 p.m., and I need to dump my next dose before midnight. You need to get out of here."

"Are you going to be, okay?"

"I'll be fine. Go!"

A scratching metal sound from the living room alerted the two men. A key was turning in the lock.

"Quick! Go hide behind the bed!"

Tim threw the pill, flushed it, and went back to his bed. The stench of the cigarette burning in the ashtray floated throughout the apartment.

Frank could smell the weak smell of tacos and went to the bedroom to check on Tim. He heard a bump from behind the bed and started toward it. Tim bolted out of the room and ran to the bathroom.

Doc laid quietly, hoping no one could hear his heart pounding in his chest. Tim vomited into the toilet, and Frank shut the door to have more room.

"What brought this on?" Frank bent over Tim to brace his convulsing body.

"I don't know. I haven't had a cigarette for a while, and I felt better, so I lit up. Maybe it was the combination of the smoke and the morphine that didn't settle well."

"I smelled tacos when I came in. Did you eat?"

"I did, because I took my next dose a little early and wanted something on my stomach."

"How early?"

"At 11:30, and it's now midnight, I thought that was close enough to the right time."

"No worries. I think it was in your system long enough, so you didn't throw it back up."

###

'This is my only chance.' Doc climbed from behind the bed and made his way to the front door. 'God, save me!' Doc thought as he opened the door.

The hallway was empty, so he silently walked through and closed the door behind him. Still, on the top floor, which was off-limits to everyone, he moved to the stairs and walked down to the main level.

He stood in front of his apartment, and the door slid open. His family was asleep, and Doc heaved a sigh of relief. Sitting on the sofa, he leaned back and closed his eyes.

"Where have you been?" asked Jane.

Doc shot straight up and stared at her. Thoughts flooded his consciousness as he tried to form a sentence.

Chapter 44: *She Wolf*

John could not believe the same angel on the plane made himself known. He quietly reached beside his cot and grabbed his canteen for a drink. 'Good, no snakes.' He thought.

Swirling the water in his mouth, John tried to process everything he had seen in his dream.

Right after the snake incident, a sergeant from the motor pool started a field generator and hooked up the electricity, which enabled the water pump to the well.

Running water and a flushing toilet was a significant plus besides having electricity. The hangar was heated by steam heat, and the two pot-bellied stoves' fires were allowed to die. John got up and went to the bathroom. He accidentally kicked an empty fuel can and could hear numerous clicks of army-issued Glocks filling each chamber on his way back.

"Sorry guys, it's me, John Garner." he whispered. "I accidently kicked a can in the dark."

Every soldier was combat-ready, not knowing what to expect but was in attack posture. The safety reengaged; the nine MMs returned to the holsters' safety.

“Take your flashlight next time, Garner.” said a voice from an officer’s cot, and laughter came from the rest.

Jason sat up and chuckled.

“John, old buddy, we are on high alert when on a mission. Tensions are high.”

“I didn’t want to wake anyone up with the light.” he said. “Bad idea, I guess.”

“So, you kicked the can and had half-a-dozen pistols become instantly aimed at your head.” Jason laughed. “That makes sense.”

“Go back to sleep!” chided Baker. “Why are you awake, John?”

“I had another dream. This time, the angel from the plane was here.”

Jason and Andre sat up in their cots in excited anticipation of hearing it. John took another drink of water and began.

“The angel who was on the plane with us is named Theo. He told me the reason he was there. The prince of the air found out that we were coming.

God changed our flight plans. The storm over McChord Air Force Base was God preventing us from leaving too early.”

“But why?” asked Jason. “We are going there to help with the wounded.”

“Theo told me that the devil devised a plan to rid the world of any evidence of the experiment at the school. It was called, “Operation Boom.” he replied

“Satan wanted to destroy his dirty secret. Had God not put the storm in place to delay us, Operation Boom would have killed us along with those inside the high school.”

“Wait a minute; you said high school. What do you mean?” asked Baker.

"There is a small community involved where the bombs went off that huddled the people of that community into a high school. The bombs are not widespread as the news reported.

The devil has been systematically exploding bombs but in key areas to isolate and capture those individuals living there. David lives in that community."

"Are you saying that our mission grossly overreacted on behalf of our government? It's going to make the president look stupid."

"The enemy has his minions in high places, even in our government. I'd say that it was those close to the president that convinced him to act on the devil's behalf."

"So this convoy is overkill for the extent of what is needed?" asked Andre. "What is the real casualty count?"

"Theo did not disclose the numbers, but he did tell me that it's enough to fill a high school. He also said that David did not go into the school but stayed with Billy at a safe-house close by."

"I think I know the area," Baker replied. "Billy started a gun shop and built a hunting lodge on the back side of it. I bet that is where your brother is at."

"I think you are right."

"Did he tell you anything else?" asked Jason.

"Yes. Had Theo not been on the flight with us, the plane would have broken apart in the storm."

"He was going to tell me something else but looked up to heaven and said, 'Yes Lord, and 'Not now John, I'll tell you later.'

Theo became a brilliant light and shot through the roof and disappeared. That's when I woke up."

The three laid back down, but sleep eluded them. The dream John had, circulated their thoughts, and kept their minds active.

###

The rain had let up and reduced the torrent to a drizzle. Pounding on the roof ceased. Wolves howled. As the convoy slept on, and the sound of wolf calls grew closer.

It was early morning, and the cook had turned on the stove for coffee and breakfast. As the coffee began to boil, he heard a sound behind him in the doorway. It was a female Grey wolf. Growling and posturing indicated the convoy was in her territory. Her pack was nearby waiting to attack.

The cook took a metal pan and spatula and banged the pan sending her running and the soldiers snapping awake.

"What the…?" yelled Colonel Saunders. The cook simply said,

"I had to scare away company, sir." he replied.

"I heard, growling, but I thought I was dreaming."

"No dream, sir. It was a female wolf, and she is furious that we took over her hangar. I didn't want to hurt her. I just wanted to scare her and her pack away.

"Smart move, Sergeant." replied Saunders.

"Okay, now that we all are awake, you know the drill."

Everyone moved methodically and packed away the night gear leaving the cots for seats. A line formed outside the bathroom, and those who couldn't wait stepped outside the hangar.

Soon everyone was back inside, waiting for breakfast. Those who smoked lit up outside. Cups of coffee passed through the ranks, and sugar shakers and powdered coffee creamer followed.

Scrambled eggs and bacon were on a side table where the chow line increased and decreased as rapidly as it formed. The soldiers sat by the openings at each end of the hanger eating.

"John." began Andre. "I think that it would be prudent to head for old Billy's place on the other side of the hill west of the school. That way, the officials at the school would not see our presence right away."

"Colonel," Jason said. "Why couldn't we leak to the press that we were on maneuvers and are not part of the medical team arriving?"

"I don't think either is a good idea," said John.

"The media might buy into it, but if the officials at the school do not, it could precipitate 'Operation Boom.'

I think a conspicuous presence would hinder any disposal efforts. If we are over by old Billy's, we wouldn't know until it was too late."

"I think John is right on both counts." replied Baker. "They know we are coming. They do not know when. If our presence is not in direct sight, it will allow them time to do a clean-up."

The officers discussed their next moves as the soldiers cleaned up and packed the stoves and the rest of the equipment used to stay the night.

The duce-and-a-half trucks cranked over their engines, and black smoke plumed from their exhaust stacks. Colonel Saunders keyed the walkie-talkie, and each vehicle heard theirs squawk to life.

"Let's move out." He ordered, and his driver led the way out of the hangar. The vehicles slowly exited leaving no trace of their presence behind, and the convoy turned back onto Old East Highway 25 and headed down the road toward Albuquerque.

John was relieved that they were back on the road again and one step closer to his brother David. About a half-hour later, a man was spotted standing in the middle of the road and would not budge. There beside the man was a female wolf.

Saunders gave orders for the convoy to stop. He and Baker approached the man, and the wolf growled.

"Do not come any closer!" yelled the man. "I must speak with John Garner."

John heard his name and climbed out of the jeep and walked over to Saunders and Baker. When he saw the man, he hoped it was Theo, but he was not.

"John, come forward, please." He said. "She will not hurt you."

John moved cautiously to where the man was standing. The wolf licked his hand.

"Who are you?" John asked.

"I'm a friend of the one who is protecting you.. Please walk with me a bit."

The wolf remained on guard while John and the stranger walked down the highway.

The man said, "Do not be afraid, John. The Almighty is with you."

He touched John's forehead, and John's body crumpled to the ground. Sandy and Andre started to run to John, and the wolf moved closer to them, growling, and showing her teeth.

The two stood helpless as John was taken away, by the Holy Spirit. The wolf kept them separated. All they could do was wait for the stranger and hope John was alive.

Moments later, John turned onto his side and opened his eyes. He rubbed them and picked up his sunglasses that had fallen off. Slowly he sat up.

The wolf vanished and the stranger never returned. Andrea and Sandy raced to him and quickly examined him.

"I'm alright." said John. "The Holy Spirit took me away and placed me in a beautiful garden with David."

"We didn't know what to think. The she wolf would not allow us to come near you. When the stranger touched you and you fell to the ground it looked like you died!" Sandy said.

"Yeah! And that old girl had some very impressive fangs and growls convincing us to keep our distance." said Baker.

Sandy and Andrea helped John to his feet.

Jason ran to them with a spare canteen of water and John drank half of it. Jason noticed that John looked different to him. John had repented and asked Jesus to forgive him.

"The wolf was also an angel, and she vanished the moment the Holy Spirit returned me."

"Well, that explains why she looked more intimidating," said Andrea.

"Shall we continue our mission?" asked Saunders. "And by the way, welcome to the family of God."

"I have been for years but chose to ignore God's will, that is, until now." John replied.

"David was there, and he laid his hands on my head in the presence of Jesus. All my guilt and shame vanished, and Jesus replaced it with God's joy and peace. I finally forgave myself and I'm now free."

The men walked back to the jeeps and climbed in. The convoy sped off in the direction of Albuquerque. Barely on their way again and they saw countless vehicles heading toward them, including RV's. Saunders ordered the convoy to stop again as the civilian convoy drew closer. When the two motorcades became parallel, the driver in the first RV opened his window across from the lead jeep.

Saunders spoke first.

"What's going on? Why are there so many heading out of Albuquerque?"

"You haven't heard? There is a tornado heading toward the city and we have some injured from the storm."

"We're a military medical detachment and was heading to town to help the wounded. Follow us." Saunders immediately pressed the walkie-talkie and ordered everyone back to the hanger. The stranger in the RV allowed the military convoy to turn around ahead of them and fell in behind the jeeps and the five deuce and a half's.

Chapter 45: *The Truth*

"Did you stop by and check on our boy?" asked Sims.

"Yes, I did." Frank replied. "He was throwing up and feeling really wretched."

"What brought that on?"

"That's what I asked him. He said he hadn't smoked in a couple of days and lit up. He thought that the laced smokes along with the drug set him off."

"He could be right. I counted the pills and the script said one every six to eight hours." said Frank.

"But I told him that the pain was causing him to vomit, and he had to increase his dosage to every six hours."

"Your point?" Sims asked.

"Tim has been taking the drug every eight hours, not every six hours."

"What?"

"Relax boss, I stopped by this morning at six a.m., and he had already taken the drug and was sound asleep."

"Well done, Frank" Sims replied. "How far back does this set us regarding his will?"

"Instead of three days, I would say, to be safe six days." He replied.

"It's 7:30 a.m. and I need to head back to his apartment and fix his breakfast."

"Fine but stop by the store and grab a regular pack of cigarettes for him. We don't want any extra chemicals repeating last night's drama."

"Got it." said Frank and left to do as Sims ordered.

Tim changed out of his sweats and put on pajamas. He knew Frank would soon be back and needed to feel drowsy, so he took an analgesic and went back to bed. By the time his jailer returned, Tim had drifted off to sleep.

A pack of unlaced smokes in his left hand, Frank unlocked the door and walked in. He threw the cigarettes on the coffee table and disposed of the other pack and walked into Tim's room.

He was still sleeping which gave Frank the time he needed to fix his breakfast. He felt Tim would need something less apt to make him sick, so he made him oatmeal, toast, and coffee.

Setting his food and coffee on the dining room table, Frank went back to the bedroom and bent down and nudged Tim.

"Good morning," he said. "how are you feeling this morning?"

"Sleepy and sore."

"I'd be sore too if I'd thrown up like you did. I made breakfast that will be easier on your stomach. Do you need help getting up?"

"That would be great."

"As they walked to the dining room, Tim stumbled a little to make his captor think it was the drug. He sat down in front of the food.

"Oatmeal." he said. "That's safe, Frank."

"Just in case it was those funny smokes, Mr. Sims had me pick up a pack of regular cigarettes for you until this crisis is over. They are on your coffee table."

"That was thoughtful, thank you. I'll have one later when I take my meds at 12p.m." said Tim acknowledging the new time of his next dose.

Tim finished his meal and was back in bed by 8:30. Frank approved of his climbing back into bed. It also made him think that the testing was working well.

He cleaned up the dishes and looked in on his victim one last time before he left.

The door closed and Tim waited to hear Frank walk away.

He went into the bathroom and counted out his pills and removed one and flushed it. If Frank kept to his pattern, he would not return until 11:00 or 11:30 a.m. just before time to take his next dose.

Tim was terrified and wondered how long he could pretend without being caught. He was also afraid for Doc and wondered how he was holding up with all the intrigue.

###

By the time Doc's family got up, he had breakfast sandwiches and bottled water waiting for them. He opened his water and was eating a sandwich when Jane and the kids walked into the living room.

"Good morning honey. Good morning kids, I ordered take out." he said and laughed.

"Breakfast muffins with scrambled eggs and bacon. They are quite tasty."

"Very funny," replied Jane. "I don't remember these being served in the cafeteria."

"It's a special order. I have connections. We have to eat it in here and can't tell anyone or the cook will get fired." he replied.

"We won't, will we, kids." said Jane as they scarfed down the special food.

"By the way, why were the two guards at the door?"

"You should know, you called them.!" He snapped.

"Sorry honey. They asked if I was okay and disappeared."

His suspicions of them being angels was confirmed when they did disappear in front of him.

After breakfast, the kids returned to the videogames and Jane to her sloppy love stories.

Doc found the tract that Pastor Ramone put in the bag. He sat back on the couch and began to read it.

He read about angels and how they are messengers from God. They could appear as humans or in their angelic form. But what got Doc was the fact that unless a person accepted Jesus Christ, they would die in their sin and go to hell.

God's only Son, died on the cross for the sins of the world and on the third day, was raised from the dead and seated at the right hand of God.

The tract asked a poignant question; 'Where would you go if you died tonight?'

It explained that everyone is living in a spiritual battlefield and unless they have a super-natural Savior to fight the super-natural evil, that person is incapable of winning and is destined to hell. All have sinned and fallen short of the glory of God!

Doc read the scripture, John 3:16 "For God so loved the world, that He gave his one and only Son, that whosoever believes in Him shall not perish but have everlasting life."

At that moment, Doc felt God speaking directly to him. Guilt flooded his soul and he realized he was a sinner and needed a savior.

His sin help put Jesus on the cross. It was too much to bear and broke his heart.

Tears gushed from his eyes flooding his beard and soul. He moved into the bathroom and shut the door and knelt in front of the toilet.

"Dude, I mean Jesus, please forgive me for being such a chump. I never believed that anyone could love the whole-world like you do. I'm so sorry. Please forgive me.

Come into my heart and be my Lord and Savior. I believe God raised you from the dead.

He sat on the floor and wept.

"Lord, you have been moving me to this moment all along, haven't you."

Doc closed his eyes and could see in his soul two angels, who had been waiting for this moment, lift a heavy sea chest from his shoulders. It was the weight of his sin.

His heart flooded with an incredible sense of love. Peace and joy enveloped his spirit.

The final statement in the tract simply read. "If you accepted Jesus into your heart, you are now a new creature in Christ. The old person is dead. You have been born again! Rejoice! For yours is the kingdom of heaven!"

While Doc was thanking God, he received the Holy Spirit and began praying in tongues. He raised his hands to heaven and rejoiced.

The bathroom door opened, and Jane stood in the doorway.

"Honey are you feeling, okay?" she asked. "I could hear you crying and then laughing and then speaking some sort of gibberish."

'God help me.' He thought. 'Should I tell her everything?'

'The time is now.' said the Holy Spirit. 'Tell her. She will listen.'

"Jane, please come into the living room. I have to share something important with you. It could mean our lives." He said and locked the door.

"Kids, come out here please."

They moved to the sofa and his family looked at him as if another lecture is coming. His track-record with his family was not a good one. Doc had been self-absorbed all his life. Now he had to convince his family, that he was no longer the same person.

"Two days ago, I noticed some things that seemed peculiar to me. My background being a medic kicked in. It seemed like every time the people inside here, us included, ate or drank anything, we became sluggish and tired."

"Okay Doc, so what? As a former medic, you also know that going through a major trauma can also cause the same feelings."

'God give me the right words.' He thought and continued.

"Initially yes, but after time emotions level off, correct?"

"Yes, I guess so."

"Then why after days from the trauma is everyone still acting and behaving tired and lethargic?"

"That's a good question."

"Didn't you wonder why you were always hungry, always tired and never satisfied?" he asked knowing he had his family's attention.

"Honey, drugs are used by food manufacturers to kill the 'I'm not hungry' hormone in our bodies to keep us eating. Have you ever sat and downed a huge bag of potato chips and wonder how you could have eaten all of it?"

"Of course, I have." and the kids agreed.

"I have some very disturbing information regarding the bombs, the high school and the emotions of everyone here." "We are being drugged.

I've been getting food and water from a pastor who was standing outside the gate.

A couple of days ago, I took donuts out to Pastor Ramone. He had the food tested. The food in here is chalked full of drugs!" "Jane did you hear me? "She turned ashen and said, "I'm pregnant." and passed out.

Chapter 46: *Strange Message!*

Back at the hangar, John speed dialed Julie's phone again. No signal. He slid his cell phone in his back pocket and walked back inside the hangar.

A mess line was forming at the other end of the table, and he wasn't sure he could eat.

'How do I not worry, Lord?' he thought and got in line.

Jason was holding two plates of food and was heading toward John. He took a plate and stepped out of line. "Coffee is coming up in a minute."

The two joined Saunders and Baker outside at one of the tables set up. Creamer and sugar were already there, and air pots of coffee were brought out. Condiments were also set on the tables.

Cold cuts with bread and cheese along with fruit and vegetables accompanied each plate. Bottled water was also in abundance and a water truck was included in the convoy for the vehicles and cleanup.

The others were already eating so John quietly said grace and put together his sandwich.

John did you get a hold of Julie?" asked Jason

"Briefly," he replied, "and while we were talking, the signal went dead. I tried to call her right back, but it still read no signal."

He took a bite of his sandwich and fixed his coffee between bites.

"It could be the tornado disrupting service. A lot of static electricity is in the air." said Baker. "At least she knows you're okay, right?"

"That's about all I could tell her before the call went dead."

"At least you were able to reach her." He replied. "I remember when cell phones first came out.

They were called bricks because of their size. There were only so many signals and often calls were lost because the call got bumped."

"Before my time." said Jason and the four men laughed.

"I'm glad its 2019 and that issue was solved." said Saunders.

"However, I don't think they will ever be able to stop interference from severe weather. Since cell technology operates from signals that travel through the air, disruption is almost a given."

"You would think since it is 2019, the issue of weather disruption would also be conquered." said John.

"For the most, part they have been, but with severe weather such as hurricanes, storms and tornados, there is an extremely large amount of electromagnetic disturbances in the air which effectively break cell transmissions.

John sat and listened. Everything Saunders stated is true, but it did not help him feel any easier not being able to talk with Julie.

'I pray she isn't worried.' He thought. 'Julie always worries when I'm away.'

A message popped on his phone. There was no cell number or text address from where it came. It read,

"I'm Coming!"

"What in the world?" he shouted scaring everyone around him.

"What is wrong with you?" asked Jason. "You scared the heck out of us!"

John was staring at his cell phone and Jason grabbed it from his hand and read it.

"Oh boy! This is weird!"

"What's going on?" asked Baker.

Jason showed him the message and Colonel Baker didn't know what to think.

All the events have been so bazaar in the past couple of days,' he thought 'Maybe it could have been a message from God. That's crazy! Still.'

"John, I don't think it's from Julie."

"I know for a fact it's not. We have had some pretty close calls in the past, but she has never sent a message like this one or tried to come to me."

###

"John! John! Are you there?" she yelled into her cell phone. "God, what is going on!"

Katrina came out from the kitchen and saw Julie trying to redial John's number. The call fell off and read, no signal.

"What's wrong?" asked Katrina.

"I was talking to John, and all of a sudden the call went dead!"

"Could his phone have lost its charge? Mr. John is always forgetting to charge his phone."

"I know, Katrina, but that is because at home, I'm always the one making sure his phone is charged. When he is out of town, he never forgets."

"Try calling someone else to see if it is your phone."

"Good idea. Thank you, Katrina." said Julie and called Katie.

"Hi Katie? Have you heard from Jason at all?"

"Not really, he normally doesn't call me unless something happened. Why do you ask?"

"John always stays in touch with me. This morning he called me and during the call the phone went dead, and I lost the call."

"Is that something to worry about?"

"Katie, he said they haven't even reached the location where David is! I tried to ask him when the phone called died."

"Strange. Would you like me to stay with you for a few days?"

"That would be great! How soon can you get here?"

"I've a few things to button up here, and I can be there in the early evening, traffic allowing."

"Thank you, Katie." said Julie and ended the call.

Julie did not know what to do, but she couldn't call the kids. They would just worry, and she had no information to give them about Uncle David. She decided to wait.

Julie and Katie had not gotten together for months. They took turns staying with each other when their husbands were gone.

Seattle, Washington is one-hour behind Albuquerque, New Mexico, so it was only 11:30 a.m. Julie returned to the studio and cleaned up her paints. She would not be doing anymore painting today.

Julie sat down on the sofa and tried to read Sunset Magazine, which is a publication of the Seattle area and the Pacific Northwest. It was her favorite magazine to browse through and find new ways for decorating and gardening.

Her eyes drifted to the T.V. remote. She put the magazine down and pressed the power button. The screen blazed to life and a weather alert came on. Julie sat in disbelief.

"There hasn't been a tornado in Albuquerque since 1971 and one is now raging down toward the city." said the anchor man.

"Ladies and gentlemen, I've just received a report that this tornado is an EF 4!"

Julie screamed and Katrina ran into the living room.

"What's wrong Miss Julie?"

"John is heading into a tornado!" she cried.

"An EF 4 means that the wind speed is over two-hundred miles per hour. It has not touched down yet, and the nearest estimation is around one hour. We will keep you updated on KING 5 News in Seattle."

Julie's phone beeped and saw Katie was calling her.

"Hi Katie, are you leaving yet?"

"No." she replied. "I don't know what is happening, but the base has been put on alert and no one can leave or enter the base until further notice."

"Katie, what is going on? I just saw on the news that a tornado is heading toward Albuquerque right where our boys are going!" There was silence as the call went dead. Julie looked at her phone and saw a message. It read,

"I'm Coming!"

Katie looked at her phone and the message read,

"I'm Coming!"

Chapter 47: *Secret Garden*

David looked out the window and said,

"Wait!"

Everyone looked out and saw what David was staring at.

It was a giant angel holding a golden rope around the funnel of the tornado. He shook it back and forth causing the tornado to bounce and skip across the landscape. All the places it touched seared the ground leaving patches of debris behind. The angel saw Billy's lodge and secret shelter and bowed to them causing the tornado to lift above them and completely miss the lodge and the surrounding buildings.

A man dressed in white linen appeared in the common room.

"Why do you look outside at what is happening?" he asked.

"What do you mean?" asked Billy.

"The angel with the whirlwind you saw "is what is going to take place soon. Do not fear what the Lord God Almighty has planned." said the messenger dressed in white Linen and he disappeared.

Everyone was visibly shaken. They all knelt and thanked God for showing them there is no reason to be afraid. But to see a messenger from God, in the flesh, was quite overwhelming. It was 12:00 p.m. and the events were vividly imprinted on their hearts.

"I need a drink!" teased Billy. "Coffee!" he smiled and eased the excited tension in the room. He looked outside and there was no sign of hail, the tornado, or the destruction it had left. It was a vision meant for all to witness.

"David if this is what your visions are like, I can't imagine how you are able to talk about them afterwards." said Jerry. "I am amazed!"

For the next hour, the whole team talked about their experience and shared what it meant personally. There was a consensus that God was about to unfold a mighty plan against the prince of this world that would set back his evil agenda by months if not years.

###

"Now that Harry our horticulturist is here, it's time for you David, to see level three." said Billy. "Shall we?"

Everyone else had been to the lower levels and it was nothing new to them. Still, it was fun to see the excitement on a new face. The seven crowded into the elevator and went to the lower third floor.

When the doors opened, David was astonished to see hydroponics that stretched the entire length of the floor. Walls, ceilings, and floors lit up with motion.

Climate controls kept the hydroponic gardens at seventy-three◦. Workers from the church were busy cleaning off the dead foliage and checking blossoms and harvesting crops that were ready. Seasonal crops like strawberries, tomatoes, and such were able to produce all year round.

For now, the crops help to feed the church family and the church's foodbank which supplies seniors with the nutrients they need but couldn't afford.

"Every plant is organic with no pesticides and only my natural fertilizers are utilized." said Harry.

"What do you think, David? I've been working on this project for years and have developed natural nutrients used in the growing process."

Harry pulled a fresh strawberry and handed it to David. A washbasin was handy for washing and snacking on the fruit. David took the sweet morsel and tasted it.

"It's incredible!" he replied and popped the rest of the berry in his mouth.

"In the latter part of the twentieth century, the government tampered with science creating a genetically modified organism aka gmo's, which was the first organic patent in the United Sates. The company began mass producing the plants, mainly wheat and corn at first. It was supposed to be the world's answer to hunger."

"I remember reading about it in school." David replied. "What happened?"

"Almost everything has GMOs now, but later people started getting sick from it. Antibiotics were used to counteract the E-coli virus introduced to the outer shell of the DNA strand to weaken the DNA chain of the plant. A pesticide was injected into the strand to theoretically make the plant heartier and less appetizing to insects. Then antibiotics were used to kill the E-Coli. Now it is far more difficult to use antibiotics to treat infections and diseases because they are resistant to them.

"That's why God let us see the vision!" David replied. "After the rapture, there is going to be only a few pure food sources in the area; maybe even the region!"

"I hadn't thought of that David, but I think you are absolutely right!" said Billy.

"Think about it, why don't antibiotics work anymore? It's because we have had so much of it in our bodies for so many years, the bacteria attacking our systems are resistant to them. We can't escape it. It's in the foods we eat; in vegetables, in fruit, and even in our meat!"

"That's why I went to work importing seeds from other countries where GMOs are not allowed. It took a while to stockpile enough for this underground Eden, so that the food here would be safe to eat.

Even air pollutants damage crops. This is another reason for the underground garden. The only viable solution was to create a place to grow things free from any contaminates." said Harry. "It's our secret gardens."

God showed Jerry how to bring natural sunlight into the gardens by way of mini-shafts which allows the sunlight in through windows that intensify the rays.

Everyone was awed by the genius behind the food source displayed in front of them.

"I never lose my enthusiasm for this place." said Jeffery. "As a chef, I want to use all-natural products in my cooking."

"We come to this garden on a regular basis to gather fresh produce for the meals Jeffery prepares. It's like we have our own grocery store." said Tracy.

"God's grocery store." said Billy. "This is only temporary for us. The real miracle will be when the Tribulation Saints come here to live."

"It will be their secret hideout from the dark forces of this world." said Jerry. "From here, they will be able to spread the Lord's word and have safety."

"What about being followed by the enemy?" asked Gennicy.

"Have you taken into account that all believers during the tribulation will be targeted for death?"

"That's my baby," said Billy. "Your mom and I worked on a device that scrambles thermal heat signatures and produces an animal signature instead. We dubbed it H.I.S."

"Cute dad, but what does it mean?" asked Genn. "How big is it?"

"You'll love this; your mom came up with the acronym. 'Heat Intentional Scrambler.' said Billy.

"You see the smart watches we all have? They're also scramblers."

"How does it work?" asked David.

"Your personal codes you received are also the activating codes for your watch.

Key in your primary code and you can choose what thermal trace you wish to be.

Any animal you select will be your heat signature and it will not register your human one."

"Very clever!" said David.

###

"Please excuse us, Tracy and I need to pick some produce for the kitchen and will have snacks set out in about half-an-hour. It's 2:00 p.m. and we have to prep the food for dinner."

The two grabbed baskets choosing what to take upstairs and entered the elevator. The rest of the group continued to walk around the immense garden.

Outside the sky darkened, and lightning raced across the horizon. Thunder banged like two mountain goats head butting. Winds blew bending trees and shrubs unable to withstand the force. The ground shook and buildings swayed.

"Quake!" yelled Harry.

Chapter 48: *Hanger Triage*

The team watched the civilian convoy as hundreds of cars, truck, vans, RVs, and campers streamed down the road to safety. Drivers with injured noticed the army tents with white crosses on them and pulled off the highway seeking medical attention. A triage tent was erected by the hangar and the traffic was directed to park on the tarmac away from the tents. More vehicles stopped.

###

The population of Albuquerque is enormous, and John knew that the odds of David being among the escapees would be a miracle. He also felt in his spirit that David was fine, wherever he was. John had peace to attend the sick and injured. His professional and gentle demeanor reassured the patients he treated that all would be well.

After seven hours tending to the wounded, the team finally sent the last patients on their way to Santi Fe. The cook had prepared dinner and those still waiting to eat straggled in from the Med-tent and washed up for their meal. Coffee is a given beverage in the military. It was a welcome sight.

"It's a miracle we didn't have to med-evac anyone out of here." said John, as he waited in the mess line. "No compound fractures, or punctured lungs."

"I saw a few possible fractures but without the availability of X-rays, I had to immobilize their injuries and send them to the emergency room in Santi Fe." Jason said.

The four sat at the table just outside the hangar and ate their spaghetti dinner. Bottled water was handed out and everyone rested from the stress of the past few hours.

The enlisted personnel went through the area and collected the trash and policed the outer perimeter for trash and or snakes.

An area fifty feet surrounding the hangar was cleared of sagebrush and low growing plants, anything that would entice a rattlesnake to hide under.

"John," asked Baker, have you heard from Julie?"

John looked at his phone. There were no messages from anyone.

"No, I'll call her in a few minutes." He said. "I'm sure she has heard about the earthquake by now."

###

Katie tried calling Julie again. The phone rang once, twice, and then a voice came on the other end of the phone.

"Julie?"

"Katie thank God, I reached you! Did you see the news?"

"Yes, I did. Listen, the fort has removed the high alert status, so I can now leave the base." She hesitated.

"I'm sure our boys are okay. We live in an earthquake zone, so they know what to do."

"I know." replied Julie. "Any more messages, I mean, you know…"

"Right, the 'I'm Coming' message? No, I haven't, have you?"

"Me neither. I'm in my car heading out the main gate of Fort Lewis. I'll be at your house in a couple of hours."

"Got to go, John is calling." replied Julie and switched to his call before Katie could say goodbye.

"John, honey, are you ok?" asked Julie her voice thick with worry.

"Sweetheart I'm fine. I knew you'd be worried, so I called."

"Have you made it to Albuquerque yet?"

"Not yet. I have so many wonderful things to tell you. David is fine."

"How could you know that?"

"The Holy Spirit told me."

"What?"

"I'm not the same old…"

"angry all the time man?"

"Yeah, that one." he said and laughed.

"How! What happened! Did you…" Julie looked at her phone. The called ended. The message read,

"I'm Coming!"

"Sorry, I entered a dead zone for cell service, and I lost your call."

"Julie?" Katie's phone rang and she switched it to hands free.

"Katie? Sorry I had to hang up on you." John was calling."

"I hit a dead zone before you told me that John was calling. I'm at the 38th St. exit on I-5, just passing the Tacoma Mall. Traffic is moving steady, and I haven't hit the usual bottlenecks of backups yet. The first one is Fife over by Enchanted Village and the rest stop."

"That's a horrible area. The traffic often slows to a parking lot so to speak."

"I don't know what to think about John's call."

"Why, what's going on, Julie?"

"He said they are fine. Then he started talking about wonderful things he wanted to share with me. I asked him about David, and he said he's fine."

"Is that so unusual? When John is in pro-mode, he is always reassuring and upbeat." replied Katie.

"I know. When he puts on his doctor hat, he ensures his patients that everything is going to be okay."

"Jason does the same thing. That doesn't really seem out of character, does it?"

"No, but when I asked him how he knew David was okay, he said the Holy Spirit told him!"

"What?"

"That's what I asked him!" Julie replied.

"Listen Julie, we both accepted Jesus into our hearts years ago. Didn't you always say that you were praying that John would find Jesus and change his heart as well?"

"Yes, I did and I'm still praying for him. But to hear from his lips that the Holy Spirit told him David is okay, made the hair on the back of my neck bristle."

"What's the problem Julie, we always knew that the Holy Spirit is from God?"

"Katie, you know how John is, or was like. I also know that the Holy Spirit is powerful but for my John to utter such words and say he is at peace with it. Well, it's a miracle!"

"I'd say, it is something to celebrate. Julie. Julie!" 'Oh great, now what?' she thought.

She looked down at her cell phone and the message read,

"I'm Coming!"

###

Tim looked at his watch. Saturday night came quickly. It was 5:45pm., and he rushed into the bedroom and dawned his pajamas he had worn all night.

He heard the key in the front door and quickly went into the bathroom and locked the door behind him.

Frank walked to Tim's bedroom. He looked across the hall and saw the bathroom light seeping through under the door. He knocked and waited for a response. He didn't answer.

"Tim are you okay?" asked Frank. "It's almost time for your meds…"

"I'm on it. I'll be out in a second."

"Mr. Sims scheduled your doctor to come and remove your staples from your scalp at 6:30. p.m."

"Finally!" Tim replied and flushed the pain pill down the toilet. He took and analgesic from the medicine cabinet and made sure he shut the door hard for Frank to hear.

Satisfied, Frank went into the kitchen and began dinner for his captive. It would be a simple meal. Tim had frozen entrees in the freezer, so when he didn't feel like cooking or was out late and didn't want a lot of clean up afterward, he would pop one in the microwave.

Frank grabbed a Salisbury steak with mashed potatoes and gravy. He also found a side dish of frozen vegetables. He wanted Tim's medication to take affect quickly before the doctor arrived to remove the staples. The lighter the meal, the less likely it would interfere with the sedation.

It was 6:15 and Tim was starting to feel the effects of his analgesic and not the experimental drug he was supposed to be taking. He sat down at the dining table just as Frank brought in his dinner.

Frank went back into the kitchen and cleaned away wrappers and boxes from the meal and washed down the counters.

It was also an excuse to observe Tim's behavior without being obvious. Frank brought him a glass of milk and watched him.

"I thought you might like some milk."

"Thanks a lot, Frank." Tim took a large gulp.

"I'll be so glad to get this hardware out of my scalp. Maybe I will sleep better."

"I cannot imagine how you slept at all with those things stuck in your scalp."

"I think my medication helped a lot… I would be lost without it."

"Very possible, you received some really strong stuff."

"Is there any dessert? I'm in the mood for something sweet…"

"I'll check in the refrigerator."

Frank went into the kitchen and found a piece of chocolate cake in the fridge. He took the plastic wrap off and grabbed a fork and gave it to Tim.

"One of my favorites. Thanks."

The doorbell chimed. Frank walked to the front door and opened it. Sims and the doctor from the basement were standing in the hall waiting to come in. The three walked into the living room and the doctor set up a tray to remove Tim's staples.

"Are you ready my boy?" asked Sims.

"Am I ever! These things have been hurting since I got them! Boy, that medication sure helped me to sleep even though I was hurting."

"Let's make you feel better." said the doctor.

"If you will lie down with your head on the arm rest, we'll have those staples out quick."

Lying back on the sofa, the doctor draped Tim's head with a surgical covering and washed the area. He set to work extracting each staple with ease.

He noticed a bump on the ninth one and snapped the middle of it to remove the pieces from each side of the incision.

Tim screamed as blood and pus gushed from the wound. The doctor scrambled to get gauze packing and pressed it against the inflamed sight.

"Sorry Tim, sometimes a staple can make the area angry and infected. Are you okay?"

"Yeah. I guess. I just wasn't expecting anything to really hurt. Good thing I took my medication before you got here."

"At least I won't have to medicate you. I'll clean it up and put some medicated ointment in it. It should be okay in a day or two. I will leave the tube with you."

He finished dressing Tim's scalp and checked Tim's eyes and blood pressure.

"Isaiah, thank you so much for taking diligent care of me."

"Of course," he replied. "Get some sleep. I'll check on you tomorrow."

Sims and the would-be doctor left the apartment with Frank following them into the hall.

"His sensitivity levels are higher than they would be without the drug. But his eyes and blood pressure are good indicators that he needs a little longer at the present dose before we implement a higher one."

The doctor walked away down the hall toward the elevator.

"The High Council will not be pleased with the delays." said Frank, leaving Mr. Sims in the hall alone and perplexed.

###

Doc finished flushing the last of the contaminated food from the cafeteria and returned to the living room where his family was.

His silence during dinner had them worried. Jane was wondering about the health of her baby.

"Doc, what is happening around here and why were you so quiet at dinner?"

"I have to share with you and the kids the dream I had last night."

"You never mentioned anything about a dream when we got up." she replied.

"I wasn't sure I should at that point." he replied, still hesitant.

The kids were looking at him puzzled and wanted to play video games but were more intrigued by their dad's dream. Thomas and Stacey always loved a delightful story especially when dad was the one telling it.

Jane and the kids settled back in their seats and readied themselves for a fantastic tale.

"You must not tell anyone what you are about to hear, agreed?" he began. They nodded.

"Last night, while I was drifting into a gentle slumber, God came to me in a dream."

Doc took a drink from his untainted bottled water, more to give him extra time to put his dream into words.

"Sitting in what looked like a large stadium, I was in the center of it. There were thousands of people around me. I was the main focal point. Everyone was looking to me for something; words of encouragement, I guess." He took another drink.

"There were so many people. I felt like the throng was crushing me. I knew the Lord was with me and as I moved to escape the crowd, I found myself in some sort of vehicle."

An angel landed on top of the transport, as it moved backward, and he poured out what looked like a breakfast cereal on top of the rig.

It was an endless flow spilling out of the vial onto the hood and trunk sliding off onto the ground."

"That doesn't sound like anything special." said Jane. "Breakfast cereal?"

"Wait," he said and continued. "I looked, and the Lord was sitting there with me. I asked Him.

"Lord, who are the ones crowding around me?"

"They are the fallen ones trying to destroy you."

"You mean demons?" I asked.

"Why are they eating up the cereal that the angel is pouring out?"

"The demons are hungry for whatever they can get from you."

"I still don't understand, Lord. How can they crave cereal?"

"To you it looks like cereal, but you are pouring out scripture and the demons are ravenous and will ingest anything without regard to what it is. Their lusts and greed have blinded them to the content."

"I'm really confused! Isn't Your holy scriptures poison to them?"

"It is and will destroy them from within."

"Lord, is that why they hopped off the vehicle in order to fight for the so-called food falling from it?"

"Yes." replied Jesus. "There is more you need to know. Whenever My Father's words are spoken or read out loud the enemy has absolutely no power to resist it. He must flee and has no choice."

"Lord, I am a baby Christian and You saved me less than twenty-four hours ago. How have I been speaking scripture?"

"The very moment you received Me, you also received My power and authority to battle here on earth and in the heavenly realms.

You have been so hungry for the kingdom of God that all the verses you learned in Sunday school when you were a child you never lost. The difference is now you have the wisdom and authority to use them."

"So, every time I read, pray, or speak the words from the Bible, I am releasing God's power?"

"Yes, and so much more. God's children, new believers and old ones do not realize the power they are wielding when the Father's word is spoken.

Remember when I was in the wilderness and Satan tempted Me for forty-days and forty nights?"

"That must have been horrible!"

"The devil tried to trip Me up by taking the words about Me and twisting them.

'If you are the Son of God.' I always answered him by saying,

'It is written.' He knows I am the Christ and still he tried to get Me to sin! I refused!"

"I then woke up and we spoke for some time." said Doc.

"Jesus finished by telling me that until I accepted Him as my personal Lord and Savior, Satan couldn't care less about me. Now that I (we) got saved the devil is extremely scared and will send demons to derail us from speaking God's word."

"Wow, daddy! You got to see Jesus?" asked Stacey. "Does He have long hair and a beard?" She climbed into her daddy's lap.

"Does He wear a dress too?"

"That's dumb!" said Thomas. "Boys don't wear dresses!"

"Jesus had on a robe," Doc replied. "Thomas, your sister doesn't know what a robe is. Cut her some slack, okay?" and hugged them both.

"Okay you two, it's 8:30 and you need to go brush your teeth and get ready for bed." He said and kissed them both on their foreheads.

"You don't have to go to bed yet, just get ready."

They went down the hallway racing to the bathroom to see who got to use it first. Thomas let Stacey win.

"I won!" she squealed."

Jane smiled a motherly smile and Thomas disappeared into his bedroom to change into his pajamas.

She moved over and sat by Doc squeezing his arm and hugging him. A soft knock at the door alerted them both.

The door slid open. Tim stood dressed in his blue sweats and hoody, smiling.

He entered and the door shut behind him.

Doc locked the door from the inside.

Chapter 49: *Rescued*

It was 3:30 a.m. Sunday morning. Lights flashed and the computer initiated emergency protocols. Lights dimmed, the steel doors rolled down over the balcony windows and the outbuildings and lodge were secured.

"All personnel prepare for extensive weather damage." The computer said.

Everyone still in their pajamas, raced to their designated assignments. Jerry took the stairs down to the communication center and watched the monitors which the computer had already turned on. The tornado headed directly for them and had already passed the high school.

Tracy and Jeffery removed hanging pots and pans. They placed butcher knives, steak knives, and any other sharp kitchen tool which could cause harm, into a lower drawer with a lock on it.

David and Gennicy set up triage equipment in the common room. Harry was leading those from the bedroom levels upstairs.

Billy instructed the computer to bring up a visual on the balcony windows. The outside cameras sent the feed directly back to the computer in real-time showing the destructive power outside.

Everyone witnessed the funnel jumping back and forth rising above the buildings and touching down again. Marble size hail pounded the steel coverings on the windows. Lightning streaked across the sky's canopy.

In less than five minutes, the angry funnel moved away, and the air was calm again. The seven of them remembered the angel with the golden lasso harnessing the direction of its destruction. They stood in awe.

"Okay people. Head back downstairs and assess the damages." said Billy.

Those staying on the lower residential levels returned to their rooms. The damage was mostly superficial.

A few tiles on the floor were cracked, and the hydroponic pumps needed to be primed and turned back on.

Jerry returned to the common room and had the computer cancel the emergency protocol. The window coverings withdrew back into safety position and the lighting returned to normal.

###

The clattering of the marble-sized hail banged against the metal hangar. It was 4 am and everyone jerked awake. The lightning shot across the sky illuminating the tornado heading toward the hangar. It was a mile away and all the soldiers scurried to pack the deuce-and-a-half's, with all the gear.

Those who could crawled under the vehicles for protection. Others grabbed steel pillars holding on as tight as they could.

The hangar was flooding with debris, hailstones, and prayers.

Believers prayed and glorified God and nonbelievers prayed in desperation to hopefully live.

Theo stood outside the hangar and at the last possible moment before the hangar fell apart, he pointed upward and said,

"Enough! Begone! Thank You, Father God!"

John looked out from under a jeep and saw Theo and gave him a huge smile. Theo smiled back, winked, and then disappeared. The storm was over.

The personnel slowly came from their hiding places, shaking, dirty, and some of them needing a smoke.

Sandy, Andrea, Jason, and John stood by the lead jeep holding back their snickering.

"Did I hear some men screaming like girls?" asked Saunders and laughed even though some of the soldiers were women.

The group also laughed, and the tensions began to drop. One of the male soldiers said,

"Colonel Saunders. I did sir, but how do you fight this kind of enemy with a bullet or grenade?"

"Well stated soldier. Everyone here felt the same, and you can't fight it except by prayer."

"Is everyone okay? Do we have any injured?" asked Baker.

Bruises, abrasions, and minor lacerations were the final tally. The small injuries were patched up and the convoy loaded up.

"Alright people, it's obvious that this was the tornado that was to slam Albuquerque and the medical mission is now more urgent. Let's move out and get there as quickly as possible."

The convoy left the hangar and disregarded the speed limits to save time and lives.

Jason couldn't help but notice John's perm-grin. John looked at him and winked.

"What's up? Jason asked.

"I saw Theo standing outside the hangar during the storm. and we smiled at each other."

He said, "Enough! Begone! Thank You, Father God!"

then he winked, he disappeared, and the tornado was gone."

"That's awesome! Boy wait till dad hears about this!" he said and praised God.

###

Doc and Tim shared how each had come to the Lord. They were happy for each other. The hail interrupted their testimonies.

Two angels appeared in the apartment and shielded the windows from broken glass and other debris darting across the room. At two hundred plus miles per hour, even a toothpick could pierce through the body.

The five of them laid on the floor and were instructed to remain there until it was over. None of them had ever seen such large angels much less any angels.

Stacy cried and Thomas was trembling. Doc tried to hold all of them and reassured them it would be over soon and that the angels were here to keep them safe.

Tim was scared but thankful he had accepted the Lord Jesus hours earlier. He thought that if he died now, at least he would be with his mom in heaven. The thought of hell terrified him.

The angels disappeared, the storm had moved on, and all the doors to the apartments slid open. All the windows in the school shattered, leaving fragments inside and out.

People slowly left their apartments and walked outside and saw debris everywhere.

A dozen ambulances were outside along with several fire engines, EMTs, doctors, and nurses from the neighboring hospitals were helping the wounded.

Pastor Ramone and other pastors and church members searched for the more seriously injured and directed the medical staff to them.

Crashing sounds startled everyone as the five deuce-and-a-half's pushed over the cyclone fences. Soldiers poured out of the back of the trucks in full battle gear entering the school, attack ready and quickly evacuating the people inside.

The bomb squad headed straight to the basement to disarm the World War II bombs set to explode. There were three devices wired together to simultaneously detonate remotely by cell phone.

After they were neutralized, the danger was still present, and the explosive bombs were carefully removed by the bomb specialists. They were taken to the designated sight, to discharge them safely.

Billy and his team and medical staff arrived shortly after and joined in searching for those wounded. All the people that were inside the school who had been drugged with scopolamine were directed to a specific vehicle for blood testing.

John and David saw each other and ran and embraced. Tears flowed freely and both thanked God for everything.

David returned to helping Gennicy, but John did not want to break their embrace. However, his doctor mode kicked in and he joined the other medical teams.

Billy and Andrea hugged each other and were relieved they were fine. Both told the other how God kept assuring them that everything would be okay. Sandy also hugged Billy and was happy to see him well.

The local media heard the news about the scandal with the bombs and swarmed like locust to the high school, trying to devour every morsel of information spread around, from the believers outside the school.

Police were called to create a large barricade away from the school. It forced the news media back due to the volatile danger still inside.

###

Frank went to Tim's room to kill him, but he was not there. He looked in the bathroom and bedroom. Grayson was nowhere. He called Damon and reported the unfortunate events unfolding.

"I understand…" said Frank. "Yes sir, I'll go to Sims office after I change my appearance. Will do."

Frank went into the bathroom and flushed the rest of the pills. He found scissors, shaving cream, and a razor. After he cut his ponytail off, he shaved his beard and head and removed the brown contacts he had been wearing.

He changed into a pair of green scrubs and dawned a white lab coat that said, Dr. F. Smith.

In the living room, he noticed a Jesus tract sitting on Tim's coffee table.

'That explains his disappearance.' He thought and picked up the pamphlet and stuck it in his lab coat pocket.

He walked down the hall and opened Sims door and walked in. Sims had just finished snorting two lines of cocaine. The drug hit him quickly and he laid back in his chair enjoying his high.

"Frank, what are you doing here? I thought Damon gave you a new assignment."

"He did. Have you seen Tim this morning?"

"No, I haven't, I was just going to go down there. Do you want to go with me?"

"Don't bother, he's no longer there." said Frank and threw the Jesus track on Sims' desk.

"How?"

"You tell me." Frank replied and pulled out his 9mm and screwed a silencer onto the end of it.

"What do you think you are doing, Frank? I am calling Damon!"

"No need to Isaiah. You are my new assignment, ordered by Damon."

"This must be a mistake! Let me explain."

"Explain what, that you failed the High Council, and that the test run has gone public?"

Frank's demon was feeding on Sims's fear. He walked to the side of his desk and his demon groaned an order to Sims's demon.

"I cannot move! Please let me explain!"

Frank put on a pair of blue latex gloves and wiped his prints from the weapon. He placed the pistol in Sims's left hand.

"No!"

Sims' demon forced his index finger to pull the trigger and a bullet discharged into his temple and Isaiah Sims slumped over.

The demon emerged from the body and was seething with anger.

"Why did you kill my host?"

"I didn't kill him! You did! Report back to headquarters. You already have another assignment!" Frank ordered.

"Why should I listen to you?"

"Now! Or I will vanquish you!" the demon showed his face through Frank's.

"Fine!" said the little demon and disappeared through the broken window leaving an orange vaper behind.

Frank had blood on his hands and cleaned off only part of it off, so it would appear that he was helping the wounded.

He went downstairs and mingled among the medical personnel. The shortage of ambulances forced multiple injured to share the same emergency vehicles. Frank moved toward the first ambulance.

Since Adams kids couldn't go in the ambulance, Pastor Ramone had a church member drive Stacy and Thomas to meet Jane and Doc at the hospital. Jane's pregnancy made her a priority to get to the hospital quickly.

Doc, Jane, and Timothy were inside the first ambulance, and drove away as Frank walked up to it, with Frank not knowing he just missed Tim.

Another ambulance was getting ready to leave and he hopped on board posing as a doctor. At the hospital, he climbed out of the ambulance and headed toward the doctor's parking lot.

He pulled off the gloves and pressed the button to unlock his grey 2019 sedan.

He called Damon and reported that Sims was dead and to deposit his fee in his offshore account. While he spoke, the phone went dead. Frank looked at the phone and the message read:

"I'm Coming!"

"Stupid demons! Whatever!" he said and threw the disposable cell phone out the window and drove away.

A stranger watching picked up the phone. He saw the message through the fractured glass. Frank's demon saw the angel and groaned with anger.

"Perfect, Father. Right on schedule." Theo said and became a bright light and disappeared.

Epilogue

Hours past as the wounded was routed through to the hospitals in Albuquerque. The Red Cross was dispatched and took those from the damaged community to a temporary shelter, at a neighboring school a few miles away.

Cafeteria tables replaced the triage cots in the first aid tent. The cook and staff went to work setting up the kitchen for the dinner meal in the mess tent.

The other personnel policed and sanitized the tents and surrounding areas, searching for medical tools, bandages, and used materials to be disposed of in red hazardous material containers.

A special detachment from Homeland Security removed the computer equipment from the war room, and the medical materials from the hidden hospital in the basement.

The Coroner's office waited for the forensic team to release Sims' body so he could be transported to the hospital morgue for an autopsy.

The white powder residue in and around his nostrils suggested Sims to be a cocaine addict and as a result, he took his own life. But the coroner would never know about the demon who killed him.

###

Coffee, creamer, and sugar was the first order of business. Billy's team sat across from Baker's team, and Pastor Ramone and the other pastors and church members filtered inside the tent.

The air pots of coffee, creamer, and sugar moved quickly down the rows of tables as new air pots were brought to replace the empty ones. The low hum of everyone talking filled the air. Then Billy stood up and all fell silent.

"Brothers and sisters, I cannot thank you enough for all your prayers and help. We all know that this is just the beginning what the enemy has planned. It is imperative to stay alert and keep praying."

"Billy is right. What has happened here today has been in planning for a long time, maybe months, or even years! We also know that the devil is not going to stop and that the past few days was just a test run to capture and destroy as many nonbelievers as possible!" said Pastor Ramone.

"This shows us that God is in control and that the rapture is extremely close. If anyone present here today is not a believer, please, reach out and seek someone who can bring you into the kingdom of God. Now is the time to accept Jesus Christ as your Lord and Savior. Believe me. Your life depends on it!"

Billy and Ramone sat down, and the chatter resumed. Pastors were handing out Jesus tracts and many wanted to talk and ask questions about what had happened and why.

They were shocked to hear that the recent events had been devised by the devil. Many accepted Jesus but most had thought the devil was nothing more than a concept or a scary bedtime story. Now they know he is real and fear him even more.

Gennicy sat next to Billy sipping her coffee and held David's hand who sat on her other side.

"Uncle Carlos, when do you think the rapture will happen? We know it has to be close."

"It's closer than we can imagine. Only God knows. But there are several events that must take place before the church is removed."

"What about the message people are receiving on their cell phones? asked John.

"You mean the one that says, "I'm Coming!" said Andrea.

"As a military man, I think it could mean different things to different people." said Billy.

"We know as Christians it can mean only one thing; Jesus is on His way to take us home. As to a scientist, it could mean communications from extraterrestrials."

"You mean UFOs? Come on daddy, you don't believe all that junk." said Gennicy and laughed.

"Of course not. But you can't dispute all the sightings which have occurred since the 1940's. These events and even the so called abductions have been preparing the world for one thing: that it may explain away the rapture.

Time is getting shorter, and these sightings have been happening more frequently."

"There are also those who believe in a lot of fake religions. And what about the Jewish nation? Won't they believe that the Messiah, antichrist, will be sending the message?" asked Tracy.

"I believe the message, is a wake-up call for the entire world. For Jews, Gentiles, and all nonbelievers. Only God knows who will believe where the message comes from and what it truly means.

The message is for such a time as this, look up, for your redemption is drawing near." said John.

"Come quickly, Lord Jesus!" said Pastor Ramone.

And everyone said.

"Amen!"

Wake up! I am coming quickly! Be on your guard, for you do not know the hour or the day when I come. Yes!

I'm Coming!

Invitation

Beloved, if you have received this book, there is a reason you have it. Someone loved you enough to give it to you. God does not mean anyone to perish. He has given each one of us an opportunity for salvation.

If you do not know the Lord Jesus Christ, now is your chance to receive Him as your Lord and Savior. We are all sinners and need a Savior.

John 3:16 says, "For God so loved the world, that He gave His only begotten Son, that whoever believes in Him shall not perish but have everlasting life."

He is waiting for You. Why not receive Jesus into your heart right now? Say this simple prayer:

"Lord, I am a sinner and need a Savior. Forgive me right now; I confess my sins and give them to you. I believe in my heart that You died on the cross and shed Your blood for my sins.

God raised you from the dead on the third day. Jesus, come into my heart and be my Lord and Savior. Thank You for saving me. In Jesus name, Amen."

Congratulations! You just became a child of the living God! All heaven is rejoicing! Now, tell everyone you know, especially your Christian friends. They will rejoice with you.

Other Books by: J. Karon Roberts

Available on: Amazon.com

With Just His Word: Inspirational Poetry
Released March 2021

Devil's Breath Series Book 1
Released: October 2021

I'm Coming! Book 2
Release date Mid-Spring 2022

With Just His Name: Jesus
Release Date: Summer 2022

About the Author

J. Karon Roberts was born on March 2,1952, eight mile outside of Kent, Washington. She had marvelous adventures growing up on ten acres with her two brothers and twin sister.

Ms. Roberts raised three children:; one boy who is the oldest, and two daughters, and not twins. She has thirteen grandchildren, and eight great-grandchildren who are spread out across the country.

The empty nest has allowed her to pursue her life-long dream of becoming a writer. So at the age of fifty eight, Ms. Roberts returned to school. She graduated May 5, 2013, from Ashford University with a B.A. in Journalism and Mass Communication at the age of sixty-one.

Her first book. "With Just His Word" was published in March 2021 and was written during the Covid-19 pandemic. Currently, Ms. Roberts is publishing her novel series. The first book, "Devil's Breath," will be released in October of this year. The second book will launch in the middle of spring. Books three and four will launch in 2022-2023.

Ms. Roberts relocated to Montana in 2017. After living in Missoula, she moved to Drummond for a more peaceful lifestyle which she had as a child. She is now living her dream.

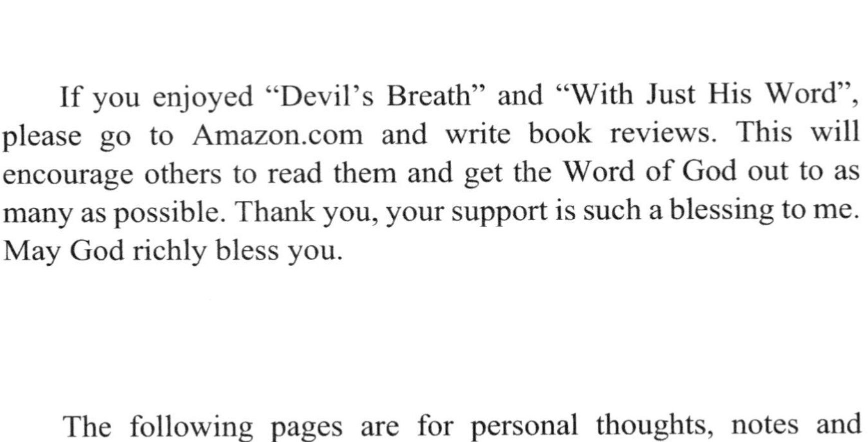

If you enjoyed "Devil's Breath" and "With Just His Word", please go to Amazon.com and write book reviews. This will encourage others to read them and get the Word of God out to as many as possible. Thank you, your support is such a blessing to me. May God richly bless you.

The following pages are for personal thoughts, notes and scriptures that you might think of while reading.

Notes and Scriptures

Notes and Scriptures

Notes and Scriptures

Notes and Scriptures